Omega's REIGN

Omega's REIGN

SAINT VISTA PACK REGIMES: PLATINUM SHORES PACK

by

GINNA MORAN

ISBN 978-1-951314-96-5 (paperback)
ISBN 978-1-951314-97-2 (hardcover)

This is a work of fiction. All of the characters, organizations, and events portrayed in this novel are either products of the author's imagination or are used fictitiously.

Cover design by Silver Starlight Designs
Cover images copyright Depositphotos

For Inquiries Contact:

Sunny Palms Press
www.sunnypalmspress.com
www.GinnaMoran.com

Omegas Must Bow

HOLLY

My brutal father would lose his shit if he saw me now. Fortunately, the cruel bastard lies as a pile of cremains in the family mausoleum far from my territory and kingdom.

My kingdom.

Sometimes—most times—I still can't believe it.

No omega in my lifetime has ever taken a leadership position within the Saint Vista Pack Regimes, and here I sit, spread eagle on my ornate throne with one of my beta boyfriends buried between my legs.

"Come for me, my queen," Jordan murmurs, peeking up at me. "Just one more time. Stop thinking. Just feel."

He knows me too well.

He calls this a brain break and loves getting on his knees when he thinks I could use a little stress relief. And I can't deny how much I need the distraction.

"I don't think I can," I whisper, clutching onto the arms of my throne, wiggling on the velvet seat.

"You can do anything," he says, adjusting his hand to slide a finger inside me. "Especially with me here, worshipping your beautiful body."

I grip his hair at the sensation, scooting forward a bit until I squeeze his head between my thighs. He growls at my sudden control, the vibration of his lips exactly what I need to lose myself. A wave of pleasure burns through me, blossoming from my clit and sizzling across every pulsing muscle.

"Mmm. My perfect queen. You're so good." Jordan shifts forward, resting his head on my lap, letting me comb my fingers through his soft brown hair. I love when he gets all bossy, especially since he's a beta and doesn't really get the chance with his older alpha brother around.

"And you're incredible. Exactly what I need." Locking my fingers to his wrists, I pull him until he gives in and gets to his feet. I adjust my dress to fall over my knees, ignoring the fact that my panties sit on top of my heels on the floor. No one is allowed in here without my permission anyway.

"Does this mean you're ready to return to the ballroom?" Jordan clasps my hands in his, coaxing me to stand.

I remain heavy in place, using my dead-weight to glue myself to the throne. "Why bother? None of the pack leaders respect me. They only ever address Beckett. They treat me like I'm here for show and to appease the Pack Regimes."

"Which is why it's important that you make an appearance and let it be known that you're our territory leader. If they talk over you, then yell. Show them who you really are. You're not the docile daughter of a dead king. You're better fit to be leader than any of them."

God, I needed this peptalk. If only every single one of his words of encouragement didn't always vanish the second I get within a foot of the cocky alphas. They're used to a cruel ruler who cares so little about anyone apart from wealth and carnal need. That's not me.

"Now come on. I'll be right beside you. Promise." Jordan tugs my hands again, and I relent, giving into his handsome smile.

I stand tall on my tiptoes and kiss him, catching the scent of our lust permeating from his skin. He should wash his face, but he won't. Not now. Not before we have to enter a room full of alphas who think they're the only ones deserving of an omega.

And Jordan has never broken a promise.

It's what gets me moving, tightening my fingers through his as we walk together down the long, empty aisle of a throne room I've never allowed anyone except for my most trusted people to visit. It's my safe space with one known entrance and then a secret exit into some tunnels built by Jordan and the rest of the Silverstein Pack. There's something about the ornate throne and pews for sitting that brings me peace. It's the place I meditate best and where I'm reminded that my life is real.

I'm an omega queen. The only omega queen.

What I do in my kingdom from here on out will set precedence for other territories. If I can prove that my rule will help people thrive, then maybe I can help encourage natural change without wars. Without force.

Because the Pack Regimes of Saint Vista have lost enough.

The territories within the region of Saint Vista have been at war. It's how I became the ruler and leader of Platinum Shores, which was formerly part of the Calico Proper region, and now in Saint Vista. I was born into the Gilded Sands Pack, and they helped start the revolution. My brothers' love of an omega changed things. For everyone. For me.

And now it's my turn to do the same.

I agreed to help this territory with the Silverstein Pack as a way to build my own path. I have lived in the shadows of my brothers for all of my short adult life. They need to focus on their territory and pack. Their family. I just want to focus on the world. On me.

Bellowing laughter pulls me from my thoughts, and I straighten my dress and square my shoulders, wishing I would have grabbed my heels to make me taller. It's easier to demand attention when I'm at the same level as the alphas within my territory instead of them looking down at me due to my size. I'm not short, but I'm not as tall as most of the alphas. However, I can be in the right heels.

I glance over my shoulder, deciding against turning around. If I return to the throne, I might not leave the safety of my sanctuary for another hour. The longer I take, the longer the alphas stay. The longer my pack has to suffer by being courteous to those who don't think we are good enough yet.

But they're going to quickly learn exactly what kind of power I have.

Jordan picks up his pace at the sight of the arched entryway to the dining hall. He wants to enter before me, ensuring it's safe to do so. I let him lead, swinging our hands back and forth, wishing I could just return to my room. I never thought I'd be such a recluse after being hidden from my father before his death. He tried to use me to gain power outside of Saint Vista by offering me to a malicious pack. My brothers disapproved of the pack our father had chosen for me, knowing how awful Righteous Waters treated omegas, and they helped me fake my death to escape my fate. They blamed Righteous Waters, framing them for my supposed murder, so we wouldn't have to worry about them. Now with my father dead and the power shift to us, it guarantees it. No one can decide on my mates except for me.

And I chose the Silversteins.

My heart races at the sight of the rest of my pack, gathered at the table with a handful of men and one woman—those who are alphas and leaders within the Platinum Shores territory. There were a few dozen after the Pack Regimes' reorganization with the cruelest of them all dead like my father, but those alphas were stripped of power by me and the Silversteins with the backing of the new leaders of Saint Vista and all the territories within it.

"Announcing Her Majesty," Jordan says, calling attention from the room.

The alphas get to their feet but don't bow as they would for someone else. I try not to let it get to me—it's been engrained in their very instincts to disregard an omega, especially one bonded with another pack—and they've been taught not to approach or speak to me.

I hate it.

Despite being an omega, I'm not used to it. These customs should be banished, and this has to be where it starts.

"Thank you for your patience. I needed a clear head before this conversation. I know that things are happening quickly and are unfamiliar to you all, considering who your former leader of the Pack Regimes was, so I want to get this over with now. I need a census done for each of your areas with every alpha and omega. All packs must be interviewed, and then my trusted counsel will help me make the final decision for whether or not your omegas are safe, in good health, and actually want to be with their packs. We're no longer allowing buying and trading to strengthen your power. Omegas will come first under my reign. Do you understand?"

Heavy silence greets me, and I straighten my shoulders and walk around the long dining table within the ballroom, the same one used by the former leader of this territory. I should redecorate but refurnishing a palace of this size would take away the time I need to ensure my people get what they need.

"Hello? I asked if you understood." I stop at the head of the table, flicking my attention to Jordan before eyeing Beckett.

"When Holly speaks to you, you need to respond. We will

not tolerate this sort of disrespect. She has been placed as a leader of the Pack Regimes." Beckett growls with his words, pressing his palms to the wooden table. "Now do you understand? The census must be done immediately. You have one week."

"Yes, we understand," the twelve alphas say in unison, speaking to Beckett instead of me.

I don't know what pisses me off more. The fact that they pretend to respond to me or the fact that Beckett has to demand such things.

"Make it three days," I say, staring at an alpha to my right, one who hasn't even tried to look at me. "I want to open the Omega Haven immediately without giving anyone too much of a chance to retaliate or try to traffic their omegas out of Platinum Shores."

"Three days!" The man finally jerks his attention to me, his mouth turning downward. "That isn't nearly enough time. I police over a hundred packs. This will cause unnecessary unrest and jeopardize—"

I hold my hand up, cutting him off. "But a week is acceptable? Would you have reacted the same had Beckett demanded three days?" Because I sure as hell don't think he would've. I got under his skin with my shortening of time, using my authority to do so.

The alpha growls without voicing his admission. I know I'm right.

"If Her Majesty believes you can handle things in three days, I'd do your best to prove her right. Show her you are worthy of maintaining your position." Beckett slides his arm around my waist, addressing the group as a whole. "However, if you need more time, take the week offered. We'll evaluate things based on how well your pack completes a simple data gathering task you all should have readily available already." He turns his head to me, closing the space, his heady scent of spice and citrus wafting over my senses. "Anything else, Your Majesty?" he asks, his voice deepening with the softness of his whisper.

It's hard to be annoyed at him for keeping the situation under control. That's a "me" problem, anyway. I just want to be obeyed and respected without having an alpha constantly reiterate the fact that what I say goes.

I turn to the group. "I'd like to meet your packs' omegas again. Tomorrow. We'll have a gathering here. Do not dress them up if they don't want to. Allow them to wear whatever makes them feel comfortable. It's casual." Without waiting for them to respond, I offer my hand out to Beckett. I don't want him saying the final word or echoing my instructions.

I just want to leave.

So that's what I do.

We leave together, entrusting that the rest of the Silversteins will see the alphas out.

I don't look back.

2

Putting Alphas in Their Places

HOLLY

"I don't know whether I'm impressed or infuriated, Holly. You know we have to ease into things if we don't want any problems." Beckett crosses his arms, leaning against the doorframe to my bedroom suite. He has never come in uninvited despite how many times I've told him he's always welcome.

"If they would actually respond to me like I'm on their level, then I wouldn't have to push. You know not even one of them willingly addresses me. I don't know why I even try. My brothers were wrong. You should be head of our territory." I slump onto my bed and spread my arms out dramatically. I'm still waiting for him to get the hint that I'd rather have this conversation without space between us.

"Beckett as the leader of Platinum Shores? Fuck that." Isaiah strolls past Beckett and enters my suite without needing to be invited. Again, I look at Beckett, but he remains firm in his spot. And he says I'm the infuriating one. He's such a gentleman when I want him to be a growly, determined alpha.

"There is only one person I want to bow at the feet of, and it's you, Holls." Isaiah drops to one knee next to my bed and grabs my hand, kissing the back of it.

I roll over onto my side and smile at him, our fingers now intertwined, our lips only inches apart. But he won't kiss me. It's one of the things I so desperately want but he's waiting. He wants to sweep me off my feet. To ensure that I really want him by my side as part of the new Platinum Shores Pack. Because according to the Saint Vista Pack Regimes, he is still a Silverstein and I'm still a part of the Gilded Sands Pack, who have just acquired this territory. It won't be completely solidified until I officially accept the crown and marry. That sort of bond is what makes us an official pack of Platinum Shores.

It's still weird to me that I have a choice. That they have

to ask me for my hand and haven't yet. I think my brothers have something to do with it, but they won't admit to it. They should know better than anyone. The heart knows what it loves even before the head. And when I met the Silversteins in that tiny diner on an adventure with my brother and his omega, Kinsey, I knew these men were to be in my life. It's why they're my consorts and my advisors with the help of my brothers.

"And I'm happy to have you bow, Isaiah. Maybe you can get Beckett to do it as well." I grin and twitch my fingers, curling and uncurling them until Beckett finally steps forward, taking my silent gesture as an invitation.

He doesn't get on board though and instead pulls the chair from my empty desk and drags it closer. I have so often dreamed about having these men in my bed, but only Jordan has ever taken my flirtatious bait. I haven't really had a chance to ask any of them about it, because it seems that there's always one meeting after another, and when I do have free time, they don't.

I hope for it to change. I almost want to stop taking my suppressant pills to guarantee it. I know what I want, but I'm afraid that maybe the Silversteins don't. I have no other real explanation.

"Bowing does not show my loyalty and admiration of you,

Holly. You have told me time and time again that you want to be my equal, and that is exactly what I see you as." Beckett reaches forward and caresses his fingers through my hair, combing the light strands behind my ear. "Isn't that what you said?"

Isaiah tips his head back and laughs. Swinging his fist, he punches Beckett in the bicep. "This isn't about equality. This is about showing Holly exactly what we're willing to do for her. Plus, I hear she loves it best seeing us on our knees. Isn't that right, Holls?" He winks at me and gives me a long once-over.

Flush burns across my cheeks, knowing that he's insinuating my intimate relationship with Jordan. Beckett might know, but if he does, he doesn't comment on it. It is out of the norm for a beta, especially the younger brother of an alpha, to claim an omega before the alpha.

"It's a stress relief," I say, biting my lip between my teeth.

"Are you feeling more stress than normal?" Beckett asks, sitting up straighter in his chair, turning from stoic to concerned in a matter of seconds.

He must not know about me and Jordan, because he's obviously concerned that I'm under a lot of pressure. But it's not what Isaiah was even talking about.

I lift and drop my shoulders, flicking my attention to Isaiah and then back to Beckett. "Maybe. I just...I could use a massage. That meeting with the alphas has me tense." I soften my voice with my words.

"I can book—"

"Damn, Becks. Get your head out of your ass and look at our beautiful omega. Don't look at her as the ruler of Platinum Shores. Look at her as our sexy, strong, independent woman who just wants a little relaxation." Isaiah rests his hand on my leg, sending tingles through my body. "You sometimes have to be direct with Beckett. Maybe even whimper a little."

I puff out my bottom lip and release a small hum under my breath. "Like this?" I tease, batting my eyelashes.

Beckett purrs from deep in his chest, the noise unlike anything I've ever heard come from him, and it goes straight to my core, turning me on in an unexpected way.

"Isaiah, will you please excuse us? I need to have a private word with Holly." Beckett stands, towering over Isaiah and me. He motions toward the door. "Get Jordan and Wesley and prepare the census given to us by the Pack Regimes. I want it ready for when the alphas turn in what they have to compare and verify with our numbers."

"As long as you promise to give her that damn massage she craves," Isaiah says, stroking his fingers down to my knee until he plants his hand on the bed to push up from the floor.

He exits my suite, smiling as he turns around once and winks again. He closes the door softly, and I sit up on my bed and turn to Beckett. The concern on his face vanishes, and he flares his nostrils, inhaling a deep breath at my closeness.

"Holly..."

I don't let him gather his thoughts and lean forward, brushing my lips to his.

He eagerly accepts my affection, sliding his big hand up my neck to cup my cheek, smoothing his fingers over my skin. There's just something magical about being with Beckett—with an alpha—that I know is mine, even if we haven't bonded like I want yet.

Maybe that will change now.

Right now.

Because Beckett said he was treating me like his equal, and to him, maybe that means he wants me to act like an alpha. Push for what I want. Take what I need.

Except I'm not an alpha. I'm an omega, and all I desire is for him to treat me as such in this moment. Not like how the former Pack Regime leaders expected omegas to be treated, but how I know I should be treated—adored, cherished, given what my body wants and craves and burns for as slick dampens between my legs on my thighs. My lack of underwear only makes it worse, the tingles of lust tangling through me, begging me to lie back and expose myself. My body silently demands exactly what I want, especially when Beckett isn't quick to give in.

Gathering my dress, I hike it up and climb onto Beckett, the breeze of the fabric shifting enough to waft my scent around us.

"Holly," he murmurs, his muscles tightening and bunching, cording his muscular arms that drop to my waist, hugging me closer.

"I'm dripping for you," I say boldly, no longer holding back my reserve. "I want your knot. Give it to me."

My words coax a growl from Beckett's lips, and he smashes them harder to mine, nipping my pout between his teeth. I groan at the sensation, rocking against him until I feel the bunched-up fabric of his pants stiffen even more, allowing me to press down harder.

I reach between us and mess with the button on his dress pants, wishing the dumb thing was easier to snap free. It's taking too long. I feel as if I will explode if I don't get what I want.

Beckett breaks away from my mouth and kisses my neck. "Holly, if this is what you want—"

"I've been dying for you, Beckett. I was starting to think that maybe I was too much. This whole situation was too much. You know I've been thinking about feeling you inside me since our first night alone in this palace." My confession pours from my lips, each word more breathless than the last. "You know it also holds back the others. Only Jordan isn't following tradition."

"You've slept with Jordan?" he asks, his voice gravelly.

"Yes." I don't stop grinding against him, letting his mind wander for a moment. He doesn't sound upset, more like he's intrigued by the idea.

"He didn't tell me. I hope he's good to you. Ensuring you come first." Beckett tangles his fingers in my hair, combing them against my scalp as I finally manage to free his cock, pulling it out to thump against my bare pelvis.

We both moan so freaking loud that I'm sure the entire palace heard us. It's as if everything comes flooding out at once, our closeness bringing ecstasy even before we touch.

"I'm still aching from before the meeting," I whisper, lacing my fingers around his girth.

He sucks in a breath. "I knew I smelled him—"

Something crashes from the hallway before my window shatters. Beckett instinctively rolls off me, flying to his feet protectively. This isn't the first time someone has attacked the palace. I'm sure it won't be the last time either. It's happened at least three times since I've permanently moved in, and I'm sure one of the alphas was too upset about the task I gave them.

Reaching for my bedside table, I pull out the small gun and click off the safety. None of the alphas ever expect me to fight back, but my brothers have been training me for years. I might be a supposed docile omega, but I can use almost any weapon given to me. And now that I have grown desensitized toward attacks, and my aim is more accurate, my hands no longer shake like they used to. I don't even scream. All I do is suppress my annoyance and follow Beckett's lead.

He heads toward my closet door, the grand dressing room even more expansive than my last. It's been converted into the entry of a panic room, hidden behind racks of clothes.

The door to my suite crashes open, and I jerk my attention to one of the guards falling onto my gleaming hardwood floors, sliding across until he hits the rug. Another guard aims a gun he's not supposed to have and shoots the beta in the stomach, a gruesome wound that might be the death of him.

Without thinking, I raise my gun and shoot, the perfect accuracy taking the man out, leaving blood and brain matter sprayed across my wall.

"Get into the panic room. Now!" Beckett commands, stealing the gun from my fingers. He looks ready to rush into the hallway, leaving our loyal guard bleeding out on the floor.

But loyalty is hard to find. I need my staff and my people to know that I don't hide from danger. I don't hide from anyone.

These alphas do. That's why they send others to complete tasks that they're incapable of. The cowards.

"Scope out the hall and call for medical," I say, ignoring Beckett's pointed finger. "I'm staying with the guard."

Beckett knows better than to argue, though he responds with a deep, frustrated growl loud enough to vibrate across my skin. "God damn it, princess. That's not protocol. Your brothers—"

"Chose not to take this territory. It is mine. So do as I say." I kneel beside the sputtering guard and press my hands to his stomach.

Beckett growls again, but he doesn't stop me. He heads to the open door and peeks his head out, assessing the situation. Pulling out his phone, he murmurs into the line, but I can't hear over the cries of the beta.

"You're going to be okay. We have medical coming. Just keep your focus on me. What's your name? I don't think we've had a chance to formally meet." Because I've been isolated. The Silversteins don't trust anybody, though they have to rely on others to help with security. Unfortunately, this will probably make them even more paranoid and make them try to keep me away from the rest of the world completely. But I won't return to that life. I won't. I've spent too much time locked away and hidden because that's what my brothers thought was the best to save me from the life my father wanted to bestow on me, even knowing that it would be brutal and my existence would fall into the hands of abusive, controlling men.

"Seth," the man says, losing color with every passing second. "I don't want to die."

I keep the pressure on his stomach, trying my best to stay calm with his pleas. "You're not going to die. Medical will be here any second. I promise."

"She's right," Wesley says, his voice like an answer to my silent prayer. "I'm here. I'll get you stable as we prep for surgery. The doctors are all ready for you, Seth. You're a good man. You have done well."

Hands lock under my arms and pull me from the ground only to have Wesley and another silent beta fill my place to help the man.

"Come on, princess. Into the panic room. The threat seems to be over, but I'm not taking any more chances. That guard you shot was thoroughly vetted. Someone had to have given him a good reason to turn against us, which means they might have tried to bribe someone else. We're going to have to go into lockdown until we can interview everyone again. We need to look over the footage." Beckett presses his lips together, his frown lowering his eyebrows on his forehead.

If his emotions weren't racing, I'd argue with him. I'd fight and demand that I be present for everything, but he looks ready to throw me over his shoulder and carry me into the panic room. I know better than to make things harder. I don't have to be a brat for the sake of it. I can let him handle things. It's going to be a work in progress before I truly take the reins over our territory's security—if ever.

My focus should be on our people. It should be on the omegas. That's why I have a pack. One that will be mine forever once we make it official, and it'll be their responsibility to help see this through.

I swallow and rest my head on his shoulder, hoping that my sudden relaxation helps his nerves. It does, and he turns and rushes me toward my closet once more, pushing past the hanging clothes and into the small panic room with a couch bed, fridge and microwave, bookshelves, a small armory, and a table. It's almost like a hotel room and just big enough not to make me feel claustrophobic.

"Will you call Jordan?" I ask, knowing that Wesley and Isaiah will want to help Beckett.

"He's already on his way. We won't be long, okay? We're going to need a pack meeting to discuss what happens next. I know you wanted to have a gathering with the omegas—"

"That'll still happen. But the alphas are no longer invited. Let this be a lesson to them." I wiggle until Beckett sets me on my feet. "Those who try to play dangerous games will face dangerous losses."

And I mean it.

I'm no longer playing peacekeeper.

Things will change immediately.

Starting now.

3

Omegas Rise

HOLLY

I hold up my finger and point at Desmond, stopping him from following Kinsey into the room. "I said only omegas and female betas are welcome into this room until I say so. You sir, are neither." Grinning at my brother, I take pleasure in being able to control the situation. Because I'm one of the Pack Regime leaders and since he's in my territory, he has to follow my orders even if it annoys the hell out of him. But that's what little sisters are supposed to do. Piss off their big brothers. I know I pissed off Wilder, Arsenio, and Enzo already. They didn't even bother trying to infiltrate my little gathering. Yet they thought wrong, thinking that I'd allow Desmond to follow Kinsey.

Kinsey squeezes Desmond's hand. "It's okay. Nothing's going to happen. You'll just be bored, anyway. Why don't you take the kids for a walk? Keep Enzo from trying to take over for the Silversteins."

None of my brothers would ever admit it, but I know this is hard for them. The territory should have been Arsenio's. Even Enzo's or Desmond's, but the three of them decided to focus on creating their pack with Kinsey. And now I have a niece and nephew to love and adore. After Kinsey gets her adult time. I can tell she asked for it since the kids aren't with her now.

Desmond glowers at me, trying to intimidate me with a look. All it does is make me step closer and smack my hand against his cheek a little harder than necessary, getting my scent on his skin.

"Listen to your omega, brother. She knows what's up. Look around. You know we're fine." I wave my hand at the small group of omegas along with two of my favorite female betas, Ginger and Lilac, Beckett and Jordan's younger sisters. They talk easily with the omegas, no longer looking as nervous as when they were handed off by their alphas.

"You're lucky you're no longer in Gilded Sands. I'd be a

bigger cock block than before, little sis." Desmond ruffles his fingers through his hair and turns to Kinsey, kissing her on the forehead. "Don't plan a revolution without us, okay? You know we're in this together."

Kinsey smiles. "Of course, we are. But maybe it's time that you give us sweet, docile omegas a chance to kick some ass."

Desmond chuckles and relaxes his shoulders, the playfulness of Kinsey's words helping him to step away and back toward the door.

I don't give him the chance to stall and press my hands to his chest, pushing him until he exits the room, and I can shut the door in his face. He won't go far. I know that Kinsey said that he should take the kids for a walk, but his ass will be planted in the hallway. I'm sure Jordan will be right by his side. They might even plot how to get me to let them in.

The moment I turn around, Kinsey engulfs me in a hug, resting her chin on my shoulder as she breathes in my hair. "You know your brothers complained the entire way here? They think you're purposely doing this to annoy them." Laughter bubbles from her lips and she eases away to stare into my eyes. Her green irises brighten with her smile, and I hug her again.

"That has always been my grand plan. Take over the world just to annoy my brothers. Conceited bastards." I roll my eyes, imagining their conversation.

"I knew it, and I'm here for it," Kinsey teases, saying the words loud enough that I'm sure Desmond can hear.

A soft groan outside the office door confirms it.

Grabbing Kinsey's hand, I pull her away from the door and practically drag her toward the grand table set up with a feast large enough for alphas but sweet enough for the rest of us to enjoy. The dessert selection encompasses half of the table while the other half consists of different deli meats, cheeses, fruit, and other snacks like nuts and vegetables.

"So, it looks like everyone's here. This is my sister-in-law, Kinsey. Kinsey, these are the leading alphas' omegas. Christina, Bonnie, Gabi, Amy, and Mary. And of course, you know Ginger and Lilac." The two female betas smile at Kinsey, and Lilac motions toward the chair beside them.

She takes a seat. and I join her, sitting on the one remaining chair at the head of the table. The other omegas fall silent, just looking around and taking everything in.

"Help yourselves. I don't really have anything specific to discuss. I just wanted to meet you all again. Just talk. See how everything is going." I give each of the omegas a long look. Most of them are still young, early twenties, but two of them are older in their late thirties.

Amy purses her lips together, her features hardening with

my attempt at starting a conversation. "It was my alpha who coerced your guard. I'm sorry," she sputters, the words flying from her lips without a breath. "He doesn't agree with the Pack Regime leaders. He's trying to prove that you are incapable of a leadership position."

I sit in silence, not surprised. I expected it to be the asshole who argued about the amount of time I put into motion over the census, but it's one of the quiet alphas that has been behaving. Not behaving, actually. Amy has proven he's just been quietly plotting.

"You can't give me back to him. He will kill me because I told you." Amy wrings her hands together. "I don't want a pack. I was alone before someone kidnapped me. I was from the Gutter District, passing as a beta."

Her history sounds like Kinsey's, and I can tell that it awakens something in my sister-in-law. She grips her fingers on the table, just staring at her empty plate.

"You didn't mention this when we first met," I say, keeping my voice even. "I wish you would have. I'd have helped you sooner."

"I was scared. We all were—are. We didn't know if this was some sort of test of our loyalty set up by our alphas." Amy glances at the others.

I rest my elbows on the table, my mind whirling with a dozen thoughts. This is bad. This is really bad. "What about the rest of you?" I ask. She included them in her admission.

All of them agree with quiet nods, their faces shifting with their fear and sadness. I know I wonder if I've made a grave mistake, taking the initial word of all of the omegas in my territory. Some of them were happy—at least, I thought they were happy—to stay with her packs. But now it seems that I was wrong.

"Okay. None of you will be going back with them." I sit up straighter, and Bonnie begins to cry.

"I can't leave my pack. I want to, but I can't." Grabbing a napkin, Bonnie covers her face.

"You have children," Kinsey says, not questioning. It's obvious that having a child or someone you love will make you stay in even the worst situations for them.

I push back from my chair and stand up, my idea of an afternoon with the omegas turning from something I thought would confirm the goodness still left in the world into my worst nightmare. I don't even know how we're going to handle this without a complete fight. This territory isn't like the others. There is no loyalty.

"If you guys don't mind, I'd like to bring in my pack and my family. We can come up with a strategy together. I have an idea, but it'll be a bit complicated." My life has been one big lesson, and I unfortunately know I must teach the other omegas that same lesson now.

"Our alphas will know. They always know," Mary says, resting her head on her arms, obscuring her face.

"That's the plan. But don't worry. I'll keep you all safe. You have my word." If only I knew they believed it.

Beckett remains expressionless, listening as I whisper my words, telling him and the rest of our pack about the omega's confession. My brothers loom behind my pack, their tall presences distracting.

Wilder's expression grows harder, darker, angrier with each of my sentences. I can tell it takes everything in him not to push between Beckett and Wesley to take control of the situation. It isn't unlike him to start pissing matches with other alphas, but Beckett is the only one out of the Silversteins. He won't intervene especially after he had given Beckett the power to make these decisions by my side.

"So I think the only way we will get out of this without a huge fight or war within our territory is to fake an accident. It could be easy enough. We can act quickly. It could even be today. I've always wanted to board the Platinum Shores yacht and see more of our shores from the ocean. We could call it a family thing. The omegas and their children. We could drug the alphas we allow on board. The yacht can capsize. Burn it up. Something." This is exactly how my brothers saved me from my former soon-to-be pack. They faked my death in a fire. They put the blame on the alphas.

"Something like that will take days to plan, Holly. It's not feasible." Beckett scratches the back of his neck, his nerves clear with the presence of my brothers looming behind him. I know he worries that they'll change their minds and decide that the Silversteins aren't good enough for me.

I won't let it happen though.

"Then how about we invite the alphas to stay at the palace with their packs? We have cameras everywhere. It will keep them in control until we can enact my plan." I keep my gaze on Beckett, trying not to glance at Wilder to see if he likes my idea or not.

"That's a huge risk. Opening our palace for them to stay? I don't like it. I can't properly protect you and ensure the safety of everyone here. We don't have enough security." Beckett twists his lips to the side.

"I'm sure we can stay and help," Kinsey says, speaking up.

"No." Wilder crosses his arms over his chest. "We can't intervene unless it's absolutely necessary. All of this should go through the Pack Regime leaders for a discussion."

I place my hands on my hips. "You know that they'll tell us to let them be to maintain peace. They'll tell us that we've already changed enough, and that risking our territory isn't worth protecting a handful of omegas. Platinum Shores isn't like their territories. This one is like a pumped-up version of the Gutter District. They only kept it in place because it belongs to us." It hasn't always, but my brothers gained Platinum Shores as restitution for the atrocities caused by the former leader. "Please, there has to be something we can do immediately. I know you are concerned about our safety, but I'm capable of taking care of myself. You have seen it. My brothers have guaranteed it. Don't make me demand to have the final decision. This is important to me." Is it shitty that I basically threatened Beckett? Absolutely. I've put him in a hard position, but he doesn't understand things like I do. These omegas are terrified. They don't deserve the constant fear, and they asked me for help. That is why I agreed to take over this territory. To help omegas. Not to placate alphas. Not to be some sort of face of change. I accepted this to prove that I'm capable of ruling. I'm capable of having my own territory and helping others get the rights that they deserve. The rights that only an omega understands what it's like not to have.

"If you think this is a good decision, then I stand by you," Beckett says, straightening his back.

Wilder raises his hands. "It's not a good decision. It's—"

Arsenio and Enzo each lunge for Wilder and pull his hands down, restraining him. Enzo slaps his hand over Wilder's mouth, shutting him up before he can say something. I'm thankful for my brothers' quickness because Wilder can't always control himself. He's always been hotheaded.

"I think this will be a great thing," Isaiah says, speaking up for the first time. He, Wesley, and Jordan are usually quiet when it comes to meetings because they're used to having Beckett always lead. And it even intensifies around my brothers. They're not exactly afraid of them, but they also don't want to cause problems. "I have a few things that will keep the leaders busy. We can make this work, and quickly."

I smile at Isaiah, my heart picking up pace because he believes in me and my plan. It's not that Beckett doesn't; it's that Beckett is afraid of the risk.

But there's always a risk. There will always be something in our way.

"This will be a good thing. I swear to you. We will make it work." I hold out my arms, wiggling my fingers, and getting the rest of the Silversteins to close the space around me, engulfing me in a hug.

My brother stares at me from behind them, silent and stoic, probably a bit judgmental, but I don't care. It's not only the

Pack Regime leaders I have to prove myself to. It's also my brothers.

It's a good thing I'm up to the task. My favorite thing to do is prove them wrong.

4

HOLLY

"Beckett's mad at me, isn't he?" I sit beside Wesley in his suite. I still can't go back into mine after the guard attack. There are dozens of other rooms to choose from, but I've decided I no longer desire my own space. I've had enough of my own space to last me the rest of my life.

Wesley shrugs without replying to my question and holds up a square of fabric to my nose. "Smell this."

I can barely intake a breath before a pungent, unpleasant fragrance smacks my nose. I swing and bat the fabric away, wanting it nowhere near me. "What the hell? That was gross. Is this some kind of punishment?"

Chuckling, Wesley tugs out a second plastic bag from a duffle beside him. I missed him pulling out the first one because I've been lost in my thoughts about Beckett. "Definitely not. Smell this one next."

I lean away and shake my head. "No way. Nu-uh. Get that away from me. It smells like BO."

"I thought it was nasty too. I told Becks not to even bother with this one." Wesley pulls out yet another bag, the sight of it sending my stomach tumbling.

Sliding to the other end of the couch, I put space between us and pinch my nose. "No more. I can't stand it. Why are you trying to kill me? Death by stench was never on my list of ways I'd die." My nasally voice whines, muffled against my palm.

Again, Wesley laughs. "I swear I'm not trying to kill the woman I've fallen in love with. This is actually to help keep you safe. Now I need you to pick the one that smells the best to you."

I crinkle my forehead in confusion, staring at the stack of bagged pieces of fabric Wesley pulls from his duffel bag, no longer doing it one at a time.

It's now that I realize what's happening. I understand why some of them smell so bad to me. This isn't just some smelly fabric. They are the scents of different alphas, and Wesley is trying to make me pick one out.

"Why do I need to pick an alpha scent? You know Beckett is my alpha." I tighten my jaw, uncertainty picking up the pace of my heart.

"Of course, Beckett is your alpha. I'm not trying to replace my best friend. But we want you to be able to tolerate the scent of your new personal bodyguard. Things are getting really tough around here as we figure out who we can trust, so we have selected a handful of possibilities from Gilded Sands. Alphas that would be loyal to the soon-to-be former princess of that territory." Wesley opens up another bag. "I think you might like this one. It kind of smells like cotton candy to me."

I reluctantly stretch my neck and inhale a breath without taking the bag from his hands.

He's right. The fabric does smell like cotton candy. Maybe a hint of bubblegum. It's super sweet and pleasant.

"Nice, yeah?" Wesley asks confirming the expression he reads on my face. "Smell these three as well."

I gingerly open one bag at a time and sniff the fabric, the first one smelling like wet grass and mint. The second and third have floral notes, one of them more like honeysuckle and the other one jasmine. I like all three of them and nod my head.

"These four I can live with. But what I don't get is why? Why do you want me to have a personal bodyguard?" And how can my guys trust anyone else outside of our pack?

Wesley frowns at my question, dipping his chin slightly to break away from my gaze. He goes from playful to somber in a matter of seconds.

"I hate to admit this, but we need the help. We need someone who will be just as respected as Beckett, because Beckett can't be around you twenty-four seven if he's to take care of other duties. And no one really likes to listen to betas. It's why we are not one of the strongest packs. We have our shortcomings." Wesley finally flicks his gaze back to mine, his golden eyes not sparkling like usual.

I scoot closer to him and clasp his hand between both of mine. "You underestimate yourself. You are just as strong as any alpha I know. Maybe even stronger. You know my brother does just fine." I'm talking about Desmond, the only beta of my siblings. And I'm the only omega. We've kind of been outsiders from our family together, even though we are still close. But my alpha brothers will never understand what we have to go through, considering our orders have been considered less than for as long as anyone can really remember.

"But we are constantly being tested to prove as much, lovely." Wesley doesn't use terms of endearment often, but when he does, it always makes me giddy inside. And lovely is one of my favorites. He sounds so cute saying it.

"We just have to get through the next couple months when everything will finally settle." I lean in closer and touch my hand to his cheek, rubbing my palm over his skin, hoping my scent will fill him up with something more joyful than his intrusive thoughts about not being able to handle things.

"Which is why we would like you to have a bodyguard. Someone who can always watch out for you." Bowing closer, he brushes his lips to mine, the feathery soft lightness of his kiss sending tingles across my body. "It'll also allow the rest of us to let our guards down a bit. Not a lot but just enough to where we won't be so concerned about the outside world and we can focus more on you. On what you want and need." His insinuation gets to me in a good way, and I shiver, kissing Wesley more fervently. But he doesn't let me shower him with my affection for long.

"So what do you say? Will you accept a bodyguard?" Wesley smirks, continuing to caress my arm while holding my other hand.

"If it guarantees I can show you what you mean to me, then yes. I know you guys are hesitant, but you don't have to be. Not anymore. I want you to know that you're mine. I can't wait to make things official." Heat rises to my face, my boldness not very omega-like. I was raised to focus on my future alphas' wants and needs and not my own. I was supposed to be placid and just wait and wait for whatever to happen to actually happen. And now I can comfortably do as I please. I didn't know power was so addicting, but I understand why others fight so hard for it.

"I can't wait for that either, Holly. I know you're getting anxious, but I promise you that we have vowed our loyalty to you in this territory, and we will follow through." Wesley helps me get to my feet. "I swear on my life."

And I believe him with my very existence.

It's a promise that won't ever be broken.

"Are you sure they're okay? The alphas aren't getting angry, right?" I rub my hands over my wrists, my nerves intensifying every time I think about the omegas and their confessions. It's only been hours, and I don't know how we're going to pull off keeping them for much longer.

"The alphas are fine. Beckett has smoothed things over, saying that you'll give them an additional week to complete the census if they allow them to stay for as long as you want. He played it off like it was a way of controlling you. If you were too busy playing hostess, then you're not focused on ruling. I really think your idea about the yacht will work." Isaiah rests his hands on my shoulders, peering into my eyes. Beckett needed both Jordan and Wesley to help him arrange the excursion while also keeping the alpha leaders busy.

"I just hope we can do it soon. Tomorrow at the latest." Because any longer than that means we'd have to figure out a better excuse as to why we haven't allowed the alphas to see their omegas.

"Which is why you need to pick your bodyguard. Everyone has been vetted personally by not only us but also your brothers. They all have the skills we are looking for, so it's up to you to make the final decision, my queen." Isaiah smiles with the words. I love when he speaks to me like this. He's always quick to give me a commanding title, as if he enjoys the fact that I hold the power of our territory.

"I've already narrowed it down to four. Can you just pick? Eeny Meeny Miney Moe and all that jazz." I lift and drop my shoulders. "This is so weird to me. It kind of feels like I'm being set up on a blind date or something."

Tipping his head back, Isaiah laughs. "This is far from a date, though it is a commitment. We were just insistent that you'd pick someone that you were comfortable with. We don't want you to be creeped out. You can tell before we can whether or not someone respects you."

"Fine. Let's just get this over with. I'll do my best to pick someone who won't get on anyone's nerves. Is Beckett really behind us? You guys weren't pushy to him or anything? I can't imagine it being easy having another alpha guard me." I've already asked this question a hundred times, but I can't help wanting to be certain. The last thing I want is for Beckett to resent this. I also don't want him to think he's not good enough, when I know he is.

"Yes, Beckett came up with this idea. No, we weren't pushy. And it might not be easy, but things are never easy. Our greatest concern is you and your safety." Isaiah kisses my forehead and spins me around, nudging me toward the closed door to the library. It's the only other shared space besides the office that isn't open to the staff and the rest of the palace. It would be too hard in a bedroom to meet with a group of alphas, and there was no way I was going to just pick someone from a piece of paper. I need to meet them for myself.

"Not just for my safety. I don't want to be the one solely responsible." This weird position I found myself in was never something I even thought about.

The Silversteins are an established pack, but because they weren't formally a ruling pack, they don't have large numbers like my birth pack. Bringing in an outsider is not normal. But it has to be done. We've been bringing in a lot of outsiders, but at least we know for certain this bodyguard isn't jeopardized by past leaders like every alpha in this territory is.

"You're right. This is for all of us. Now if you need me to step in, just do the gesture." Instead of having a specific word that might sound out of the ordinary, we have decided on a secret gesture that lets all my guys know something is up. All I have to do is place my index and middle finger on my right temple. It's easy enough to remember but not something that stands out or is something that I would normally do. Not like scratching my nose or sneezing.

I bob my head and show him the gesture once before opening the door to the library. I brace myself for the collection of scents I've already experienced through the fabric pieces Wesley had brought for me. Silence greets me, but the four alphas stand up from the plush chairs arranged around a coffee table in the middle of wall-to-wall bookcases and in front of a large glass-topped desk.

Many omegas would immediately drop their gazes and take a step back, looking for one of their pack members to hide behind, but that's not me. These guys need to immediately know that I'm a queen and a member of the Saint Vista Pack Regimes. Not Isaiah. Not Beckett, Wesley, or Jordan. But me.

"Thank you for joining us today, gentlemen." I glide forward and turn my attention to the closest guy.

His ginger hair rests neatly in a perfectly parted style with a crisp fade to show off his cropped sides. Extending my hand, I proffer it to see how he reacts. This is the first test.

"My name is Holly," I say, introducing myself.

The guy glances at my fingers and then looks behind me at Isaiah.

The man across from him, and the second one closest to me, steps into my personal space and takes my hand in his. Instead of shaking it, he gently squeezes with a bow. "It is a pleasure to meet you, Your Majesty. I'm Tony."

Well, Mr. Tony. At least he passed my first test. He's not afraid to look at me or speak to me. His rose scent wafts to my nose, permeating with his closeness. His dark brown eyes rove over my face with interest, and I can't help pulling my hand away and putting space between us.

"It is nice to meet you as well." I turn to the other two guys still standing in their spots. One of them is a blond with blue eyes, freckles, and a mustache. If my memory serves me correctly, his name is Zack.

Which means that guy next to him with the shaved head and goatee must be Roger.

"My apologies for my hesitation. I'm Andrew. I didn't mean to offend you. I was just taken aback. When King Wilder contacted me, I thought he was joking about you being—"

Tony cuts him off by stepping in front of Andrew and

blocking him from me. "I was just as surprised. It has been almost two years now, hasn't it, Holly Dolly. I'm surprised you don't recognize me. Your brothers didn't either. I guess false accusations do something to an alpha."

My heart sinks into my stomach. This can't be. The flowery scent of roses crashes over me again, and I realize that his scent isn't familiar because of the fabrics. None of them smelled like roses. It was honeysuckle and jasmine. Cotton candy and bubble gum. Wet grass and mint.

"You're not Tony. You don't smell like wet grass and mint." I automatically press my index and middle finger to my temples and spin toward Isaiah who is already closing the space from his position at the door.

"Sorry about that. He wasn't good enough." The imposter tries to grab me, but Andrew locks his fingers around the back of his shirt and yanks, dragging the guy away.

Everything happened so fast. Isaiah grabs me and lifts me off my feet, carrying me toward the hallway. The window shatters as the imposter smashes through, breaking out of Andrew's reach.

An alarm rings through the air, signaling the palace to once again go on lockdown.

"Where's your panic room? I will escort you there," Andrew says, gripping the desk lamp to use as a weapon.

Tears burn my eyes. I can't focus. It feels as if I can't breathe. That man—that imposter—was part of the Righteous Waters Pack. He was one of the alphas my father had arranged for me. He was imprisoned and now he's somehow free.

And he's after me. I know it. He wants revenge.

5

JORDAN

"The intruder landed on the southside. He's making a run for it through the garden." Wesley's voice rumbles through my earpiece.

"I'll get the fucker," I growl, gripping my gun in one hand as I bolt from the sliding glass door of a guest room and across the patio.

I'm getting really fucking irritated that these assholes keep managing to bypass every damn security measure we put in place. How this alpha managed it? He had to have killed someone. He had all the right identification and looks that matched his profile. Everything checked out, which infuriates me. I knew that I should've had one of the Gilded Sands princes double-check for me, but Holly needed someone immediately. I thought I would be enough.

"He's going to jump the wall," Wesley says, his voice growing louder.

I don't respond, charging even faster, my heart racing and my muscles flexing with each thud of my boots. This guy can't get away. If he gets away, others will find out. They'll keep testing us and keep trying to steal away our power. I can't let that happen. Not because of my pack and what we want. But because of Holly. She deserves the strongest pack and protectors to help her with Platinum Shores.

We all underestimated the difficulty we would face taking charge. I have never had to be as ruthless as I am now on Holly's pack, and I really have to get my shit together. For her.

"You're catching up. He's about fifty feet east, looking for something to prop against the wall. I don't know what he was expecting. I don't think he has a weapon. He hasn't brought anything out." Just because he hasn't unveiled a weapon means nothing. I'm not going to trust him regardless.

"On it," I say, slowing down, taking to the row of trees for cover. I'm not here to just capture this fucker. I'm here to make sure he doesn't get the chance to scare Holly again. To get even within reach of her. I'm here to set an example.

My boots crunch over the dry mulch and I wince, slowing down even more, getting my gun in position. I hold it up with two hands and use it to focus my search of the rich, green grounds in front of me.

A soft groan hums through the air, and I pad my feet closer, listening to what sounds like someone straining.

I spot the intruder dropping a large cinderblock against the wall.

Without calling out or giving a warning, I pull my trigger and shoot. He ducks at the same time to adjust the cinderblock, causing me to miss, my bullet penetrating our border wall. Scrambling away, the guy uses the block as a shield, protecting his torso.

I pull the trigger again, missing his head by inches. He runs awkwardly, using the trees to his advantage.

Now, he's making a fool out of me.

"If you surrender, I won't kill you. If you don't, I will catch you and make it hurt," I call, my voice loud and grumbly with rage. The fact that he's here at all and continues to evade me really damages my confidence. If I was an alpha, I'd have him already. He'd be dead. Holly wouldn't need an extra bodyguard. Our pack would be unstoppable.

"Last chance!" I yell, darting around a tree to follow the perimeter wall. He might be a fast bastard, but he's loud as hell, which makes it easier tracking him. Our ten-foot walls aren't easy to jump over, and if I keep stalking him in this direction, he'll end up at the cliffs overlooking the Pacific Ocean. The only way out from there is down, and no one can survive such a jump with the jutting rocks below.

The intruder doesn't respond, making it his mission to piss me off. He must have a death wish or he's smart enough to realize I'm lying through my teeth. There's no way I'll let him get out of here alive. I'm done taking prisoners. Treason against my pack can have no other punishment besides the end of a life.

"Beckett is heading toward the cliffs. If you can't take him out, Beckett will. So you better hurry your ass up. Holly wants a hero." Wesley growls with the words, but his anger isn't directed at me. It's directed at the asshole running away like a coward.

"You're wrong. Holly doesn't want to hero. She wants someone to cuddle. She wants blanket forts. Orgasms."

"A big fat knot."

I glower even though he can't see me. "There are other ways to satisfy our girl." Because neither of us are alphas.

"Then you better get this fucker."

I push myself harder, running faster, knowing that if I can just close enough space I can have better accuracy. It must be a kill shot.

The familiar hum of the ocean breaks through the sound of my heavy breathing, and I use it to give me one last boost of energy. I don't think I've ever run so fast in my life, but this is for Holly. This is for our territory. I can't let everyone down, and I can't let Beckett beat me to the guy. It's always the alpha who saves the day. I need to prove that wrong.

Subtle movement in the corner of my eye draws my attention to one of the palm trees lining the cliff top with a barrier to keep people away from the edge. There that fucker is. He doesn't have the energy to keep running, so he's trying to hide, probably hoping we'll think he's gone. But no one escapes our property without our notice.

Instead of calling out to him again, I stalk him like a predator chasing prey. He won't even see this coming. It's the only mercy I will give someone. I'm not a psychopath. I'm protective. If they come into my home and try to hurt my pack, they don't stand a chance.

The blond guy crouches close to the ground, the cinderblock now resting at his feet. He has a phone in his hand, and I'm pretty sure he's texting someone. I doubt he would risk calling them.

I continue closer, wanting to make sure I hit my target in the head. Lifting my gun, I aim it. Five. Four. Three—

"Beckett ordered you not to kill him. Standdown, Jordan. We need to get information," Wesley says, his voice humming in my ear.

God damnit.

It takes everything in me to obey Beckett's order, and I clench my teeth.

"If you move, I will shoot you," I mutter, quickening my pace to close the space completely.

The guy jerks his attention to me, baring his teeth with a low growl.

"Such a tough guy, huh? How did you think this was going to end? What did you want to get out of this?" I stand firm in my place, knowing that Beckett will be here soon.

"I'm here for Holly. She belongs to my pack. I came here to let her know that we'll be coming for her. Thought it would be fun to surprise her like this." The guy smiles, a wicked grin splitting his face, sending a chill down my back. But it's not him. It's his comment.

No one claims Holly. She isn't a piece of property. She is our queen. Our leader.

"What the fuck are you—"

A loud pop sounds through the air, and the guy's head

knocks back into the tree, blood spatter spraying everywhere with the bullet hole.

I gather my bearings faster than I can process what just happened and twist, pointing my gun. Beckett stands only three feet behind me, his gun still trained on the dead man.

"Are you kidding me? You said to keep him alive. Were you just trying to be the one to punish him? I had him. You can't fucking claim this win for yourself." Anger boils through me, the surprise of Beckett shooting him sending my mind whirling like a destructive hurricane.

"Calm down, Jordy. This isn't a competition. We got the information we needed. He didn't need to live another moment, and you shouldn't enjoy getting so much blood on your hands, brother. It's my job to bear that kind of weight." Beckett tucks his gun back in his holster and stares at the dead man.

"What information? All he said was that Holly belongs to his pack. We don't even know which one that is." I clench my fingers, knowing that if I don't put my gun away, I might shoot at the dead body a couple more times. But that would be wasteful. I'll just have to swallow my anger.

Beckett wipes his hands on the front of his dress shirt. "But we do. I know exactly who they are. You know Holly's history. You know why her brothers faked her death."

The information slowly clicks together in my head like an

easy puzzle, and I try my best to remain stoic. He's referring to the pack that the former king of Gilded Sands arranged for Holly to marry into. He believed that omegas were best used to gain power, and he saw this particular brutal pack as a good ally despite their ruthless behavior. They didn't believe that omegas were to be cherished. They believed omegas were to be used. To produce offspring. And once they no longer can? The omegas are as good as dead. They can find a new one after if they want. But the most powerful packs ensure that the heirs are limited to keep power in their favor. They entrust the numbers to come from other family members. From alliances. They believe there should only be one true leader despite how many alphas stand by their sides.

The Gilded Sands princes are one of the exceptions. They rule together. Wilder, the oldest, was intended to take over the throne, but he thought it best to have his brothers equally by his side and Holly as a good ally for a territory they didn't truly want to deal with.

"Come on, Jordan. Holly has been asking for you. I'll have security take care of this guy. We will send him home as a warning. And then we will deal with that pack. Okay?" Beckett drapes his arm over my shoulders, pulling me along. I don't respond and let him, staring at the ground until we reach the concrete foundation of the terrace leading back into the palace.

Dozens of betas rush around, following Beckett's orders to ensure no one else is on the property. This might give an even better reason to keep the alphas of our territory here instead of letting them take their omegas home. Maybe this was a good thing despite the sinking feeling inside my gut. I can only handle one awful thing at a time. Holly doesn't need this kind of stress. She shouldn't have to worry about protecting omegas. They shouldn't need protection. Especially from the ones who claim them.

"She's in the panic room with Isaiah and one of the alphas who was interviewing as a bodyguard." Beckett rolls his shoulders. "I need to check on a few things. Can you handle it?"

"Handle our girl? What kind of stupid ass question is that? Of course, I can. She's all I like to handle." I don't give Beckett a chance to respond and jog away, heading toward the staircase that'll lead to the closest panic room by the library. We have dozens in this palace because we are still familiarizing ourselves with the territory, and we want our staff to also be protected. But there are only a handful that allow just Holly and the rest of our pack inside.

"Send Isaiah out when you get there," Wesley says, speaking into my earbud.

"I'll send the bodyguard too. I think we need to figure our shit out and get more verification." I turn off my communication device without waiting for a response. There's no point. I don't need permission.

All I can think about is engulfing Holly in my arms and kissing her until she forgets the trauma she's been through for even just a little while. I know better than to assume that my affection could cure her fissured soul. She's been through a lot.

I jog the rest of the way, passing a couple doors, mostly just vacant rooms, until I reach the last one in the hallway. It's not hidden or anything. It's one of the more easily accessible panic rooms, with a steel door and safety precautions such as a password, hand print scan, and retina scan. We liked to have several measures in place just in case.

The door unlocks for me, and I slowly push it open, not wanting to rush inside.

Holly jumps to her feet at the sight of me and dashes away from the small loveseat with Isaiah. A ginger-haired man stands in the corner, his broad shoulders squaring at the sight of me. He looks ready to tackle me, but he remains in place. That must be the one who was interviewing for the bodyguard position.

"Jordan, are you okay?" Holly asks, running into my arms.

I wrap her in a hug, stroking my hand along her spine. "I should be the one asking if you are okay, my queen. You must've been so scared. I have failed you. He checked out for me. I verified his identity and everything, but he must have an excellent fake ID distributor."

Holly tips her head back and looks up at me, her hazel eyes shining. "Oh no, you don't. It's not your fault. This is my fucking father's fault. We wouldn't be in this position if it weren't for him. I had no idea the Righteous Waters Pack was released from prison. They might have been imprisoned for crimes they didn't commit, but they still committed plenty of crimes that should have locked them away in the first place. They've killed people."

So have we. I don't say it though. She doesn't need to think about that kind of thing.

"We're going to take care of it. They won't hurt you, and they have no formal claim." Isaiah stands behind Holly.

Holly swallows and eases away from me. "I know. They just want to fuck with me. I'm sure they're pissed off."

"They'll learn real quick to get over it. Things have changed. They'll see. Now let Jordan take care of you for a bit. I need to check on the alphas, okay?" Isaiah says, rubbing his hand across Holly's upper back. I guess I didn't have to peel him away from her after all.

I look at the ginger man. "Thanks for your help. Beckett will give you something for your effort, but I think our pack needs to reevaluate whether or not Holly needs a body—"

"Andrew has already been hired by me, Jordy," Holly says, cutting me off. "He did an excellent job protecting us, and Wilder confirmed that he is who he says he is."

My mouth drops open at her revelation.

Isaiah pats my back. "I'll get him settled and then we'll have a meeting real soon."

I blink a few times, and Holly squeezes me, forcing my attention away from the new bodyguard and my packmate. Fuck me. Why did I even assume that I would get a say in this?

The panic room door clicks closed, leaving me alone with Holly. I bow lower, burying my face in the crook of her neck. "Are you sure about this? We can handle this."

Holly sighs and eases away, resting her palms on my cheeks. "Just because we can doesn't mean we have to. Andrew knows a lot about this territory and all of the different packs. I think he'll be a good fit and an exceptional member of our team."

I stop myself from arguing and press my lips to her forehead, ensuring she doesn't see the frustration on my face. "Yes, my queen. You're absolutely right."

If only I wasn't suddenly jealous.

Why couldn't I be an alpha?

Why can't I just be enough?

6

Power Struggle

HOLLY

I didn't expect to make it one day, let alone weeks before the alphas started asking about their omegas, but it was just enough time.

It helped that Beckett was able to make them believe that other packs were coming in to try to take their places. It's easy to forget about everything else when your power is being threatened. They're selfish enough to not even think things through. At least they believe we can handle an outside threat compared to a threat from them. Stupid alphas.

"You have to dress up, Andrew. We've decided that we won't be introducing you to them as a bodyguard. You're going to be introduced as a new member of the Silverstein Pack." Beckett holds a suit bag up. "This should fit. I've had the tailor add a dozen more to your closet. Tonight is going to be a bit complicated. I want you to meet with Wesley for a couple of minutes to ensure you understand the plan."

Andrew looks at me, waiting until I confirm that I agree with whatever task one of my guys gives him, treating me as his superior. He doesn't talk much, which is fine, but I do hope he chills out just a bit. He literally opens every door and tells me it's all clear regardless of where we are. I didn't know having a hugely buff shadow would be so distracting.

"That sounds like a good idea to me," I confirm, motioning toward Beckett's door. "We'll appear stronger that way. Welcome to my pack, Andrew."

Something changes on his face, and he silently shifts his gaze away and smirks just a little.

Beckett closes the door behind him and turns to me, his face flooding with emotions now that the other alpha is gone.

I don't even have a chance to open my mouth before Beckett presses his lips to mine, kissing me deeply, passionately, his surprising desire enough to awaken my lust.

I giggle and rest my hands on his cheeks, getting him to slow down and look at me. "Not that I'm complaining about your affection, but what's this about? Is everything okay?"

Beckett smiles with a nod. "I've just missed you."

"It's been hours."

"Feels like eternity."

His mouth finds mine again and I kiss him, sliding my tongue between his lips. His hands travel down my sides until he squeezes my ass, lifting me into his arms. I graze my tongue over his, exploring the softness of his mouth. His scent permeates around me, the tangy citrus like a breath of fresh air, and I comb my fingers into his dark hair, pulling the strands softly.

"You have no idea how much I want you, Holly. I don't know what has gotten into me, but ever since you mentioned your desires, I haven't been able to get you out of my head. I'm frustrated that all this shit has kept me from you. You're my omega. Mine." Beckett growls with his words, setting me on his bed, his sheets fragranced with everything I love about him and more.

I realize why he's gone from holding back to boldly voicing what he craves. It's because of Andrew. I'm sure the fact that he's an alpha does something to Beckett, even if it was Beckett's idea to hire an alpha bodyguard.

"You're my alpha," I say, my voice soft and sultry. "I've been waiting for this moment."

"And I have to take it. I want to take it. I regret not realizing sooner. Because if something happens tonight—"

I cut off his words with another kiss, stealing all his thoughts until he releases a guttural moan. "You're not allowed to put bad energy into the world. Everything will be perfect. I know it."

I shove him back and grab at my shirt, yanking it over my head before he has a chance. He purrs, drinking in the sight of my sheer bra, the fabric not even enough to truly support my breasts. I only wear it because it makes me feel sexy.

Beckett caresses his fingers over my hard nipple, playing with it through the lace, the sensation sending electricity from my chest, bolting across my stomach to strike me between my legs. My clit pulses at just the thought of Beckett's touch, and I reach between us and unfasten his pants. I'm afraid if I don't take control, he might start overthinking things and stop. I can't let him. I need his full attention on my body. I need him to lose himself to his deep-seated nature as an alpha. I think him doing this, being with me, claiming me, will help his insecurity over being not good enough. Because he is good enough. He's better than good.

Moaning, he rests his palms on the bed, watching me stroke his cock with both of my hands, one holding him firmly in place and the other one gliding up and down, my full attention on his tip and the pre-cum glistening.

I scoot lower between his legs, resting on my knees, and I taste him. The salty flavor is hinted with citrus, the same as his amazing scent, and I hum, feeling his cock pulse in my mouth.

He combs his fingers through my pale blond hair and pulls it, the sensation aching across my scalp in a good way as he tips my head up to meet my eyes.

"You're *my* omega," he repeats, his voice deepening. "It's my job to take care of you. Lay back. Now."

Damn.

My body reacts, the tingles crawling across my skin, leaving goosebumps behind. I automatically melt back into the bed, my body weak at the command in his voice. He's never spoken to me like this, and I had no idea how hot it would be.

"Lift up your hips." Beckett links his fingers to my pants and pulls off the stretchy fabric along with the lacy panties I wear beneath.

I pant heavy breaths with my lust, my body aching with need.

"Spread your legs," Beckett commands, kneeling in front of me, his cock still out and hard, completely ready to claim me. "Don't move. I'm going to devour you until you scream."

Again, I obey, slowly spreading my legs wider until I'm exposed completely to Beckett. His dark eyes rove over me hungrily, and he rubs his hard length, his muscles rippling with each stroke.

"Give me your knot, my alpha. I want it so badly. I can't wait any longer." A whimper escapes my mouth, and I wiggle on the bed, feeling my slick dampening my thighs.

Beckett's eyes flash with his desire, and he shakes his head, resting his palms on my knees. "Not yet. Soon. I have to taste you. I have to hear you scream my name, my beautiful omega. My love."

I arch my back and wiggle my hips, encouraging him to hurry up. I want to rush. I want to finally feel what it's like to be completely at the mercy of the alpha I'm in love with. His mercy means protection. It means love. It means everything good in this universe.

Dragging his hands down my legs and to my inner thighs, Beckett draws his thumb across my lips, spreading me open wider for him to see my clit, now aching between my legs, throbbing in anticipation. Flicking his tongue over his bottom lip, he wets his mouth, his hunger for me as potent as his alpha scent drawing me closer. Making me wetter. Tantalizing me in a way I never expected.

And I know this is nothing like it would be if I were to stop taking the suppressant pills that keep my hormones in control and help disguise me as an omega even though it is well known.

I've done it to keep my heat away because the idea of losing myself to my nature during these times of uncertainty freaks me out just a bit.

But now with my mind heavy with lust, all I can think about is what it would be like. The feeling of being insatiable. Of craving his knot on a different level than now. The idea of breeding.

Beckett's tongue pushes away my thoughts, and I tighten my muscles at the sensation, the pleasure ripping a moan from me. It's as if he already knows my body and exactly what to do to set me off.

I reach for his hair and lock it in my fingers, guiding him to stay exactly where I want until my orgasm explodes through me like a molten wave of ecstasy. I gasp and scream, knowing it's exactly what he wants to hear. It's what will push him forward to have sex with me. To give me his knot.

Beckett drags his hands up my pelvis and squeezes my breasts, fingering my nipples and rubbing them. He bites his lip, drinking me in. I breathe heavily, my mouth parted until he kisses me. I cling onto him, guiding him closer, feeling the weight of his body on mine.

His cock throbs between my legs, the soft pulse and heat of his skin zinging electric bolts to my very core.

I hook my legs around his hips, digging the heels of my feet into his bare ass, not even caring that his pants aren't all the way off. That he still wears a shirt.

With one hand, he grabs at the fabric and pulls his shirt over his head, his muscles cording in his other arm as he holds himself above me. I can barely wait. I feel as if I'll die if another second passes before he's inside me. I'm wet with my desire, my body demanding my alpha satiate me in a way I have never experienced before.

"My brother has been preparing you for this moment, hasn't he? Has he been gentle?" Beckett purrs the words, his voice vibrating across my cheek before he sucks my earlobe into his mouth. "Has he left his mark?"

I roll my hips beneath him, trying to align our bodies, silently begging him to push inside me. "He has. I'm ready for you now. I need my alpha. I want to feel your knot."

"I'll make you ache."

"That's what I want."

He growls and aligns his hard cock, pushing his tip inside, the girth thicker than his brother. I intake a sharp breath at my body stretching to accommodate him. He kisses me, slowly, gently gliding inside, my slick lubricating me in a way that it only hurts for a second before the pain turns into complete pleasure and I rock my hips, getting him to push deeper.

"You feel incredible. So damn wet. Hot." Beckett rocks his

body, gliding in and out of me, as he kisses my lips, moving to my jaw, to my neck. My shoulder tingles with his lips, and he sucks my skin, leaving a hickey.

I nip his skin, returning his affection, losing myself in everything that we are together as an omega with my alpha. With the one person who can satiate me on a deep-seated level beyond the intimacy of sex. This is more than that. This is an unbreakable connection. One we have both worked hard to create, our bodies now tangled, our minds in sync. Our hearts a perfect reflection of each other, beating in the same rhythm.

I moan and dig my nails into his back, his body pumping deeper and faster, his lips more forceful, his desire turning palpable that I feel it beyond just our devotion.

"Are you ready for my knot?" Beckett asks, slowing down just enough to help me breathe.

"Yes. Fucking yes!" I scream with a moan at the same time his cock swells between my legs, the pressure intensifying until another orgasm floods through me, triggered by his. He bites my neck hard enough to make me bleed and to remind me exactly of the pleasure he gives me.

My vision darkens, my breath hard to catch, and Beckett whispers how much he loves me. How honored he is to be my alpha. To be the one I chose. And how he could never live without me. How he will devote his entire existence to our pack and our future together.

We stay locked together, our bodies now as one and unable to part until we both get our fill. I listen to Beckett's breathing, his heart beating, and I kiss him until his knot finally releases me, his seed dripping between my legs, blending with my slick, making me all too aware of what I'm missing since I've been taking suppressants.

Now I realize how much I want a family with Beckett. With Jordan, Isaiah, and Wesley. And I have to fight for it. This was exactly what I needed to push me forward. Platinum Shores will not fall during my reign. It will thrive. We will all thrive.

Worthy

HOLLY

I squeeze Beckett's fingers, standing tall by his side as we enter the dining room. The long table is filled with both the alphas of Platinum Shores and their omegas. None of the girls look up from their plates, completely broken by the sides of the men who ensured they would be obedient breeders.

My stomach twists.

My heart aches for them.

A blip of fear steals my breath away at the realization that their lives could've been a reflection of mine. I could've been in their place.

I force the thought away. I can't think about the Righteous Waters Pack and how they managed to send one of their members to intimidate me. I should've known they'd somehow escape a lifetime imprisonment. Because what other reason would the courts—the Pack Regimes of Calico Proper—have to keep them locked away?

But I'm angry they didn't tell us. I should've been more prepared. The disrespect leaves me filled with rage unlike anything I have ever experienced. Even more so than when my father had told me exactly how little he thought of my life when he betrothed me to these wicked men who would have gotten off on seeing me suffer.

"Gentlemen, you may take your seats," I say, speaking up before Beckett can address the alphas. "I know things have been a little tense around here, but it seems that everything is in order now. The threat has been placated and we have the person responsible for the attack in our care."

My gaze falls on Amy's alpha, and I lock eyes with his. I expect him to look away, but he doesn't, trying to make me waver. Trying to intimidate me with his big, bad alphaness. But all I do is smile wider. He thinks he's won. He thinks he has gotten away with trying to kill me. And now he's going to be the one we make an example out of right in front of everyone.

This is for Amy. This is for all the omegas in this room. In our territory. I need to show the world that they are completely wrong in underestimating my ability to match brutality with my ruthlessness, born from injustice and nourished with vengeance. I have killed a man before. And I will kill again.

"He will be handled accordingly, and then we will celebrate our new circle of power between us." I keep my smile firm, my eyes locked on the bastard.

Beckett grabs a wine glass and holds it up. "Let's make a toast. To Platinum Shores and Holly."

Everyone raises their glasses.

Wesley hands me the weapon, his presence protectively behind me with Jordan and Isaiah. Andrew stands on my other side, ready to protect me if the other alphas react.

"Cheers," I say, aiming at Amy's alpha.

He doesn't get a chance to move. To beg for his life.

I get the justice we all deserve by pulling the trigger.

I am a ruthless queen when it comes to taking care of my people. I will end anyone who tries to ruin what I'm trying to create. I'll be the villain in their story if it means I'm the hero of mine.

Silence fills the room as the alphas realize that I'm not playing games. I'm not in this position just because my brothers gave it to me, and the Saint Vista Pack Regimes agreed with them. I'm in this position because I'm worthy.

"Let this be an example. I'm your leader. That will not change. It is up to you to adapt. Treason will not be tolerated. Do you understand?" I hand Wesley the gun, my fingers numb from the sensation. "My brothers raised me well. Do not forget it."

These alphas probably think I'm psychotic with how I force myself to smile. But my insides twist. The edges of my vision shadow. In a moment that's supposed to make me feel powerful, I feel weak. It makes me feel no better than them. It's funny how my feelings can just suddenly change because of the flick of my finger.

This isn't how things should be, but it is what it is right now.

I turn around and stride from the dining room, abandoning Beckett to deal with the aftermath. Andrew's soft footsteps follow behind me until he catches up and stays by my side.

"Holly, slow down," Jordan says, filling the empty space to my right. "Let me take a look at you."

I stop in my tracks and turn to face him. Glancing down the hall, I make sure I'm out of view of the arched entrance to the dining room. "We need to hurry up and finish this. I can't stand them being here a moment longer."

"Everything's ready. They won't be a problem. I can already tell you that." Jordan opens his arms, begging me to step into them.

It hurts to deny him, but I don't want to stand in this hallway any longer. "Just ensure it, please. I need a moment, okay?"

His face falls with his realization. I don't think I've ever denied him my time, but I've never killed a man in cold blood. Last time it was because I was being threatened. Because my pack was being threatened.

I feel like a monster.

Without waiting for him to argue, I cross my arms over my chest and turn away. I enter the first room I come to and try to close the door. Andrew puts his foot in the way and silently follows me in. I don't have the will to kick him out, so I ignore him and head toward the window of the unoccupied staff room.

Tears burn my eyes, and I stare out at the back lawn with a view of the ocean. The sun lowers in the sky, the sunset blazing with reds and golds, bouncing off the gilded clouds that remind me of the desert sands of my birthplace.

"You probably think I'm a mess. That I'm heartless and crazy," I say, filling the silence with my voice.

Andrew's presence doesn't allow me to ignore him, even if it isn't his intention, his cotton candy and bubble gum sweetness permeating everywhere he goes, battling with Beckett's citrus and overpowering every other scent.

He doesn't respond to my comment, remaining the stoic shadow he's been hired as.

"I should get used to this. Alphas need to know me as the bitch queen who stole everything from them," I continue, blinking the tears away but instead they splash on my cheek. "I'm sure I terrified those omegas. They probably won't even believe I'm one now."

The thud of Andrew's footsteps draw closer, but he still keeps his space, keeping to the perimeter of the room yet getting into my periphery.

"If I may speak, Your Majesty," Andrew says, surprising me with his comment.

I turn to him and meet his gaze, his green eyes vibrant in the streaks of sunlight coming into the room. "You never have to ask to speak. You might be my bodyguard, but I don't treat people like my servants. That's not how I want things to be. And call me Holly. I only allow my formal title in front of the leaders. They need the reminder that I'm in charge, because it's the only way to get this territory to a better place. Once that happens, I hope to be seen as someone for the people."

"You're a lot like your brothers, Holly," Andrew says, stepping a little bit closer.

I lift and drop my shoulders. "Maybe Desmond."

He shakes his head. "I see a lot of Wilder in you. That's the reason he thought you would make a good leader."

"He just wanted to get me out of Gilded Sands so he and my other brothers could focus on knocking up Kinsey without grossing me out all the time." Heat burns my cheeks with my words. "It was a long year with them in isolation."

"I can't even fathom what you've been through."

"It probably made me who I am. Psycho killer." I blink my eyes again, forcing away my tears. I shouldn't be this upset over murdering a monster who would have easily taken my life.

Shaking his head, Andrew turns toward the window, breaking eye contact. "You're not a psycho. And you killed that man for a good reason. I looked over all the evidence that your pack gathered to turn into the Pack Regimes. They authorized this, you know. And the fact that you are standing in this room, demanding space from your mates because you're trying to hide how much this affects you proves as much. You're afraid they'll look at you differently. I bet you're wrong. All they're going to see is the woman they're in love with. If anything, they will question why they couldn't protect you from doing that."

A smile quirks the sides of my lips, and I exhale a long breath, feeling the weight of the world lifting. "That's nice of you to say. I still feel bad."

"As you should. That was a brutal thing you had to face,

and if you didn't show your emotions, I'd truly believe you were one of those alphas. It's hard to tell your order." Is this his subtle way of asking me if I'm taking suppressants? There once was a time when they were illegal, and now they're just frowned upon mostly by alphas. But I can't give a fuck about what they think. Even if I'm starting to change my mind about taking them.

"I can't have my order distracting everyone, now can I?" I smirk wider, already feeling better. "The alphas would act way worse toward me than they already do. Now they just avoid looking at me and speaking to me. They would probably fight harder if I was distracting them with my pheromones."

"Or maybe they would finally realize that things have officially changed and only the best people get to lead despite their order." Andrew messes with his tie, loosening the fabric. I can tell he doesn't like formal attire, and he only wore a suit to meet me because that's an expectation.

"You think so?"

"Yes."

"Are you sure you're not just against suppressants? I know that it fucks with alphas."

"Absolutely not. I just don't like that people feel they have to take them. It's like—"

A knock sounds on the door, cutting off Andrew's comment. Wesley's voice rumbles through the wood, and I peek toward the door, knowing that life goes on now. I can't hide forever.

"I'm coming," I call, adjusting my dress and fixing my hair with my fingers. I turn to Andrew. "Some of us don't feel like we have to take them. Just so you know."

I straighten my shoulders and walk to the door to greet Wesley.

He gives me a long once-over, his brows scrunched on his forehead. "Are you okay, lovely?"

I bob my head. "I'm better now. Sorry about that. I just needed to gather my bearings."

He engulfs me in a hug, and I meet Andrew's gaze from over his shoulder. "I'm here for you."

"I know," I whisper. "I know."

"Cheers to Her Majesty," Vic says, raising his glass for the third time in ten minutes. The alpha took my message to heart, proving just how adaptable he is. I thought this yacht party would be super awkward and quiet, considering I just killed someone, but they have proven just how twisted they really are.

I hold up my glass and fake a sip, my stomach still a bundle of nerves. I imagine what it would be like to just drop these alphas off in the middle of the ocean and say good riddance, but then I would just have to deal with another group. When one alpha falls, another rises, and I don't see many in this territory acting much better. At least not yet.

Music hums across the sundeck, lit by twinkling lights, the soft glow like stars on the water. The city lights of Platinum Shores light up the land, and I appreciate the view from this super yacht. It takes a whole staff to manage the boat, and it's big enough to keep all of us for several days, the cabins spacious and the main suite like an apartment. It's a shame this yacht is on its final excursion. I can imagine inviting real friends aboard, my brothers and Kinsey, Beckett and Jordan's sisters. Other omegas. I wish they were here now instead of these asshole men who have lied about how they've treated their omegas. How their omegas are so terrified of them that it has come to this. We still need the alphas, but they don't need their omegas, and it's time I set them free. They will no longer be in Platinum Shores. Kinsey will help them find suitable mates at her club.

Comforting arms slide around my waist, and Isaiah rests his chin on my shoulder. It wasn't long ago that we were both giggly teens excited about this new adventure. I may only be twenty, but I feel as if I have lived a thousand lives. Isaiah has had to live twice as many to keep up with being a beta among a pack with an omega leader.

"We have about an hour. The alphas need to be drunk enough not to realize what's happening." He whispers the words, his warm breath playing with my hair. "Can I distract you until then?"

I spin around and face him, hooking my fingers around his neck, pulling him closer for a kiss. "Dance with me?" I hug him tighter, swaying to the music and taking the lead until he gives in to my desire and presses his palm to my lower back, clasping my right hand in his. He's not much of a dancer like the others, but he'll never deny me. And I love that he does this for me now.

We sway and move, the ocean breeze scenting the air with salt and the intoxicating aroma of champagne. Isaiah dances me toward the bow of the yacht and away from the small group of alphas enjoying the fresh air instead of partying in the saloon.

"Do you think we're doing the right thing?" I ask after a minute, losing myself to the sensation of cold air prickling goosebumps over my skin. "It's dangerous."

"I believe that anything we could have decided on would've been dangerous. These men aren't good. They are only compliant because they want to keep their power without a battle they can't guarantee themselves victory over." Isaiah spins me and dips me low, the quick motion making me squeal.

"I'm just afraid. What if they find out that we set this whole thing up?" Because I still can't stop thinking about the Righteous Water Pack and how they're out there somewhere, wanting revenge.

"Then they find out. The omegas will be safe regardless. We have ensured it." Isaiah slows down and stops dancing, pulling my hand to his chest, letting me feel his heart beating.

In the corner of my eye, I spot Andrew hovering nearby, protecting and promising that no one intrudes on our space. Not that anyone would right now.

"You're right—"

A scream rips through the air, disappearing on the wind. I stiffen in Isaiah's arms and swing my attention to the sundeck and where the alphas congregate. But that was a female scream, and apart from the two beta female staff members, only the omegas are women.

"I said stop!" Gabi yells, her voice clear and drawing closer.

I spot her figure running along the railing of the yacht with someone chasing behind her. It's her alpha. They step into the light shining from the side of the yacht, and I yank Isaiah away from the bow. Brutus glowers, the old alpha still fit despite his age and gray hair. And he looks pissed off.

"Shut up, Gabi. Don't make a fucking scene." Brutus

stomps forward, and one of the alphas hanging out gets up and blocks Gabi, preventing her from running.

She cries out, holding her hands up, but it doesn't stop Brutus. He jerks his arm out and grabs her by the front of the shirt, yanking her to him.

"Stop! You're hurting me! You're too drunk," Gabi cries, her voice shaking with her words.

"I don't fucking care. You will bend over for me. I'm so damn horny. Don't make me look a fool." He shoves Gabi, sending her reeling. She hits the guardrail and uses it to steady herself.

Brutus shoves her again, his anger overpowering his good senses.

I scream out. I can't believe what's happening.

Gabi falls over the guardrail and disappears into the dark ocean.

I'm afraid she'll drown.

8

Power Trip

HOLLY

"**A**re you insane?" I shout, dragging Isaiah with me as I rush to the guardrail.

A figure moves to my left, and I don't even have a chance to process Andrew leaping off the side of the yacht and into the water.

Isaiah swings his fist and punches Brutus in the face, sending his head jerking to the side. Vic stumbles from his spot and smashes a bottle of champagne, using the neck of it as a weapon. He surprises Brutus and stabs in between his shoulder blades deep enough to drop the alpha to his knees.

Wesley's familiar scent engulfs me, and a moment later I'm in his arms, being dragged away from the brewing fight and from the screams. From the crew gathered by the railing.

I can't see Gabi or Andrew, the crowd blocking my view. This wasn't supposed to happen. What if everyone demands we return to shore before we are far enough out? What if Andrew doesn't manage to get Gabi...what if he can't manage to...

I can't think about it.

"Over there!" Jordan yells, his voice dragging my attention from my dark thoughts. "He's got her over there."

Someone throws a lifesaver and two lifejackets over the edge and some of the staff race past us and head toward the back of the yacht.

My head pounds, and I shiver, the cold ocean air digging into me, mixing with my fear and anticipation.

"Take a breath, lovely. The deckhands have jet skis. They're getting them now. They're safe." Wesley adjusts me in his arms, cradling me like a blushing bride when I feel like a small, terrified baby. I shouldn't be so easily startled. So surprised.

I hate that I misjudged Brutus. No one anticipated that he'd boldly try to brutalize his omega with everyone around. My stomach twists in disgust at the thought. At how long she's lived a life under his control.

"You'll pay for this!" Brutus yells, fighting against Vic and another alpha, I don't recall his name. The broken bottleneck injured the raging alpha, leaving him bleeding, yet he still fights.

"Calm down or you're going overboard next. You know the law—"

"Fuck the law. Fuck that bitch!" Brutus points at me. "You're nothing more than a piece of pussy on a power trip. You need to be put in your goddamn place."

"Don't threaten my mate," Beckett says, growling. "You will get on your knees now. This is treason. You have disobeyed the law, and there is no forgiveness or mercy at this time."

"Are you kidding me?" Brutus struggles against the hold of the other alpha. "You can't do this. I deserve to be put in front of the Pack Regimes. Calico Proper would have never let you get away with this. You're going to destroy the damn territory. Saint Vista can't continue this way if it wants to survive. There are rumors that the other regions are plotting a hostile takeover. If you kill me, you won't get any more information."

My mouth falls agape at his revelation. No one's ever mentioned regions outside of Saint Vista. There are many others across the nation, but they've always recognized the power of each other and worked in unity to make sure these lands were always prosperous.

Beckett unholsters his gun and rests the barrel against Brutus's forehead. "Do you think we are stupid? Do you honestly believe that you would have more information about our territories and the other regions than we do?"

Brutus squeezes his eyes shut, his muscles tensing. "They see you growing weak. They saw how easy it was for the regions within Saint Vista to implode."

"And they will discover how wrong they truly are if they do try anything. You're hereby convicted of the attempted murder of an omega and treason against the leader of Platinum Shores. Your services are no longer needed. Another alpha will be put in your place." Beckett doesn't take his eyes off Brutus.

"Wait!" Brutus wails.

Beckett doesn't wait. He's already warned him that there would be no mercy, and it's our right as a leading pack to convict and punish those who break the law. Again, we must set a ruthless example until our authoritative figures finally accept the fact that it doesn't have to be this way. Or until they all fall by my pack's hands.

I close my eyes, the pop of the gunshot ringing in my ears. It steals away the commotion coming from the back of the boat until I hear Jordan call out for towels.

"Gabi," I whisper, thinking about the omega and the trauma she has had to endure. I want to be the one to tell her it's over. I want to tell her that she will no longer have to suffer under Brutus's power. She is free.

"I'll take you to her," Wesley says, adjusting me in his arms until I hook my legs around his waist.

I bury my face against the crook of his neck, breathing in his fresh scent, much softer than Beckett's. More neutral but still comforting. Like clean linen and something more powdery. A white flower, perhaps.

I keep my eyes closed until the cool breeze of the ocean dissipates and silence fills the room. The saloon remains empty, though water spots collect on the rugs in a chaotic trail leading toward a gleaming mirrored and metal elevator. I haven't seen much of the yacht, but what I have seen has been extravagant. It's almost like a palace on the water, and I imagine what it would be like to drift out to sea with just the Silversteins. How the world would be peaceful. How we could just focus on each other. Maybe my brothers weren't so wrong in denying the chance at getting their own territory and splitting the leadership position on the Pack Regimes.

Instead, they share it together, remaining in our homeland.

"It's best if you don't go with her, Wesley. The omega is shaken." Andrew's familiar voice hums in my ears, and I crane my neck to look for him.

I should've just kept my eyes to myself.

I had no idea that beneath his suit hid a muscular physique not unlike my guys. He stands just outside a cabin with only a towel slung over his hips, blocking his naked body. I don't know why I'm so surprised or why I can't take my eyes off him. It's like the tattoos that dance across his hard pecs hypnotize me. And the branches of what is some sort of tree direct me to the V of his hips, pointing to the one place I should not be staring directly at.

Wesley clears his throat and sets me on my feet. "Is that okay, Holly?" he asks, shifting on his feet, staring at the side of my face while I continue to stare at Andrew.

"Mmmhmm," I mumble, trying to convince myself that there is nothing spectacular about this alpha. About the man who is now my bodyguard. Even if his sweet, succulent scent screams otherwise.

What am I even thinking?

"I'll wait right here." Wesley touches my chin, getting me to look at him.

Flush burns my neck, sneaking up to my cheeks. I can see my red face in the reflection of a metal sconce with decorative lightbulbs. "I won't be long. I need to address the situation with the others." Again, I turn my attention back to Andrew, his quiet presence still demanding my full attention.

Wesley chuckles, his playfulness surprising me. It helps me not feel as bad as I should. "I can smell your interest," he whispers, leaning in closer. "I told Beckett that this would be a possibility."

I yank my attention away from Andrew, finally coming to my good senses. "What? What are you talking about?" We both know that I understand his insinuation.

"Beckett was fine, by the way. You don't have to worry, lovely." Wesley nudges me away, cutting me off from any more questions.

Now I'm going to have to talk to Beckett about this. To the others. Why would they even discuss such things? Andrew isn't part of the Silverstein Pack. He's hired to be my body-guard and nothing else. Beckett just wanted an alpha because they're more respected.

Holding my breath, I tiptoe past Andrew, not looking at him. He remains in his place, not bothering to move or walk away. He wouldn't anyways. His job is to stay here, even if Wesley doesn't leave either. A part of me doesn't want to go because I'm afraid they'll talk.

But why am I nervous? This is wrong. Right?

Fuck me.

I tap my knuckles on the closed door to the cabin Gabi stays in, and she lets out a soft whimper at the sound of me calling her name. Easing open the door, I peek inside and see the older woman wrapped in a robe and sitting on the edge of the bed. She twists her hands together, the tightness of her hold turning the tips of her fingers purple.

And then she begins to sob, her shoulder shaking, the rest of her body crumpling forward until she hides her face on her legs, bent over completely.

I rush to her and envelop her in my arms, pulling her close until she buries her face in the crook of my neck, her tears dampening my dress and hair.

Her emotions get the best of me, and I can't stop my eyes from sheening over with tears. It's as if I can feel her fear. Her relief. Her storming emotions filled with confusion and hope and something darker.

"You're safe," I say, wishing my voice would come out stronger. She doesn't need a whimpering omega in this moment. She needs a leader. A protector. Someone to make her feel as if her world isn't over. Because it's not. Her life is just about to begin.

I rub circles on her back for what seems like forever until she finally runs out of tears, her voice hoarse from crying. Probably from salt water and screaming.

"Brutus is dead. He cannot hurt you anymore. You're officially free. You and your children will finally be able to find a pack that deserves you. Or you can just be with them. It's up to you. You get the final say, okay?" I dry my damp cheek on my shoulder, trying to pull myself together to give Gabi the strength to do the same.

She leans away from me and takes my hand in hers, her makeup smeared, her eyes bloodshot and her hair sticky with salt. "What if I make the wrong choice? I can't survive without an alpha. I don't have a way to earn money. I don't have a pack to return home to. And I don't know if I want another alpha."

"You don't have to make these decisions immediately. We have a place for you to live and you'll be able to get everything together. No omega will be left on the streets. You'll be taken care of until you can take care of yourself. I promise." I hold her hands in mine and smile, imagining the good life she will finally get to live.

It makes everything I've been through now even more worth it. A part of me has always been a bit selfish, always just wanting to do things for me. But now that I can do things for other omegas? It's my destiny. I feel it deep in my bones. In my soul. This is how we make it work.

The brutality can't go on forever.

"I trust you," Gabi whispers, taking a deep breath to slowly push it out between her lips, her body relaxing, her muscles no longer tense.

"And I'll do whatever it takes to keep it. Now you'll find some clothing in the closets. You should get dressed. We're continuing the excursion, okay?" Because I still have the other omegas to worry about.

I leave Gabi in the cabin, feeling a lot better, knowing that she finally accepts that she's no longer in danger.

Wesley remains in the hallway with Andrew by his side, now dressed in jeans and a T-shirt, though my brain automatically remembers him and just his towel. I need to get myself together. Get some fresh air.

"The others are waiting in the saloon. Did you want to talk to Beckett before you go out there?" Wesley asks, his comment more of a suggestion.

But I don't need Beckett to tell me how to proceed or what to say. I can handle this.

I shake my head. "That's not necessary. I know exactly what I'm doing."

He nods in silence.

Andrew remains expressionless, and I can't help but wonder what he's thinking. If it's about the situation or if it's about me.

It doesn't matter.

Nothing matters at this moment except completing my mission.

Once these omegas are free of these alphas, we'll be one step closer to a perfect territory.

The world will see the greatness of my reign.

9

Change

HOLLY

"**I**s there anything the rest of you need to tell us? I'm tired of having to flex my power. At this point, I'm not even sure I should accept any of you as leaders in our territory. It might be best to just say good riddance." I stand in the middle of the saloon, facing the leather sectional while several alphas sit alongside each other. Seeing them straight-backed with their shoulders squared, eyes fixated on me for the first time that I can recall makes my skin crawl.

It used to piss me off that they wouldn't show me any attention, but now I don't want it. I don't even know what I want besides not having to worry about constant threats.

"Is this why we're here? You plan on throwing us overboard? Killing us?" Vic crosses his arms, his nostrils flaring. "I helped subdue the traitor. Isn't that worth something?"

I press my lips together without responding. Does the single act wipe away his entire history? I haven't studied his file, but I'm sure he's done stuff that would haunt my dreams.

"We're not killing anyone unless you prove that you cannot handle your current position," Beckett speaks up, drawing my attention to him. "I don't know how things were done before, but you need to quit the bullshit. Times are changing. It has been proven that treating omegas with respect and as equals makes a difference. It makes packs stronger and also helps territories thrive."

No one responds to him, remaining silent. I hope his words sink in. They can't all truly be so hardheaded that they can ignore the truth of things. Believe what they want to believe despite the evidence against them. But who knows? I don't understand a lot of things about alphas.

"This is also your one opportunity to decide whether or not you will stand beside us." I reach for Beckett's hand and slide my fingers through his. A thought rushes to me, and I can't stop myself from opening my mouth without consulting with my pack. "And I have a test to prove as much. Tonight has been enlightening. I was under the assumption that all your omegas were happy and safe. Brutus proved that to be untrue, so I have decided that you must hand over your omegas and your children until I can decide if you are worthy of them."

"You can't be serious. They'd have told you if they weren't happy." This comes from a man at the end of the couch, his features obscured with his beard. I don't recall which omega is part of his pack, but all I know is what I have been told.

"Exactly. They have told me they were happy, but it has also come to my attention that they are also scared. They were willing to say anything to keep themselves safe. From you. From all of you." It would be nice if I didn't have to go through with the plan. To sink this yacht and to send the omegas into hiding. I've experienced that life and while I was safe, I also feel as if I missed out on a lot.

"So what? If we disagree, what do you plan to do? I don't want my omega at risk. I'm the only one who can protect her." This comes from another man, one I recall being named Jonathon. He's one of the younger ones, and I'm not even sure his omega has gone into heat in his pack.

I exhale a breath, my sigh loosening my bunched muscles. "This isn't something you can agree or disagree with. It's happening."

The guy on the end of the couch stands up. "You can't do this! We have done everything you have asked. We have stood down and shut up about all these stupid little changes you've made. We have ensured that the citizens in our areas have complied. We've separated families. We've cut off alphas from their packs. Everyone is fucking miserable, and it's your fault. The only reason I have agreed to this nonsense is because my omega was still mine. But if you take her—"

"She's not your fucking property!" Jordan snaps, speaking up for the first time. It's unlike him to lash out, especially in front of the alphas. He usually lets Beckett handle all the communication. "You don't have control over her."

"The hell I—"

Bright light floods in through the floor-to-ceiling windows, stealing my attention away from the grumbling alphas. I shield my eyes, realizing that another vessel has pulled up alongside ours, and whoever man's the boat shines a spotlight on ours. It's much smaller, and I can't see it from my spot. Why didn't the crew say anything? Wouldn't they have known that we weren't alone in these waters?

A pit forms in my stomach. This is bad. We're nearly defenseless. It's not like we have the protection of our palace. We're on a yacht far from land.

"Get her to the captain's suite," Beckett says, his voice

booming through the air, commanding Andrew even though he's already reaching for me.

I yank out of his reach. "I'm not going to hide and wait for an attack. Give me a weapon. Whoever it is probably wants to seize our vessel."

"Do you think it's pirates?" Vic asks, standing from his seat. He glances around the saloon, assessing the situation. They're all unarmed. We don't allow weapons in our presence just in case they try to use them against us.

"Isaiah, unload the armory." Beckett ignores Vic, turning to our packmate. "Jordan, take the omegas into the cabins. Try to keep them calm."

"Everyone, arm up. Don't try anything stupid. We don't know who these assholes are." Wesley hands me a gun and a knife, and I adjust the holster around my shoulder. He doesn't let Beckett argue with me and instead takes control as his second in command.

"Holly, don't leave my side. We need to confront the threat head-on." Beckett stands tall and looks at Andrew. "Protect her at all costs. If anyone even looks at her, kill them."

His command vibrates across my body, Beckett's authority sexy yet intimidating. I know he's not happy with my decision, but it must be this way. We all knew there was a risk accepting this position.

"Send a distress call to Gilded Sands. Tell them our coordinates." Beckett hands Wesley a bulky phone. I'm assuming it's a satellite one that can ensure our message reaches my brothers. He turns to the other alphas. "One of you needs to barricade the cockpit. No one gets in."

I try to suppress the nerves bunching my stomach, everyone getting into place. The yacht rocks on the ocean, and I watch through the glass window as a rope ladder snags on the guardrail, a small anchor locking it to the metal bars.

Rushing past me, Beckett enters the side deck and saws a serrated knife across the rope of the anchor, sending the ladder falling back to where it came from.

He points his gun toward the sky and fires, the sound of the gunshot ringing in my ears. "We are armed!" he hollers, the deep baritone of his voice shouting over the waves. "Do not board this vessel."

Only the roar of the ocean fills the air, the silence of everyone else deafening. I expect another ladder to be hooked to the side of our yacht. I didn't expect the intruders to back off. Maybe they've come to their senses. Maybe they realize we aren't just some ordinary people out for a nighttime cruise.

Beckett's chest rises and falls as he listens to the world around us, the door to the saloon open, letting in the cool breeze.

"Get behind me," Andrew says, his whisper tickling my ear. He steps in front of me like he believes I might argue, but I don't. I can't move a muscle, my focus solely on the unnerving quiet.

Beckett squares his shoulders and shuffles forward, his footsteps quieter than the pounding of my heart. He slowly closes the space to the guardrail, preparing to assess the situation.

A spotlight glows from his right, illuminating him in a golden halo. He shields his eyes and shoots his gun with one hand, not bothering to wait. If the intruders are on our boat, they aren't here on good terms.

Charging at the door, Beckett slides inside and slams it, locking it. It must be more than he can handle, or the spotlight just makes it impossible to know what's going on. I'm glad he's not the type to rush into battle without a plan. There's a reason my brothers trust him and the Silverstein Pack.

"Holly, get out of here. Do not argue," Beckett commands, his sharp voice like a slap in the face. It's not often that he demands something of me with the expectation that I'd follow without resisting.

It must be bad. Really fucking bad. I don't know if I've ever seen Beckett so wide-eyed. Scared. I can smell his citrus scent radiating with his perspiration.

"This is a hostile takeover, and we will not comply. Do you

guys understand? Shoot on sight. We will not be taking any prisoners." Beckett points his gun at the glass door, staring at the deck glowing in the spotlight.

Again, no one appears. If I didn't know any better, I'd think this was some sort of sick joke to mess with my head. That maybe one of the alphas decided to fuck around out of hatred.

"Have the captain draw the anchor. We're heading back to shore." Beckett taps his ear, talking through his communication device.

I should've known things wouldn't go as planned. Brutus should've been my first warning sign. Maybe this is a good thing. I've already made my decision clear about the omegas to these alphas. And maybe seeing how incredible Beckett and the rest of my pack handle the situation might finally get them in line. There is no better way to bring people together than a common enemy, and whoever is hiding on our yacht is the biggest threat.

"Holly," Beckett says, drawing my attention from my thoughts. "I said to go. Hide. This is not a fight you need to participate in. Trust that I can handle it."

He's asking me to step down as our leader, at least, for a little while.

I thin my lips and nod my head, giving in to the desperation in his voice, knowing that his biggest concern in life is my safety. He's not the type to willingly risk my life despite my position on the Pack Regimes. And I get it. This is more than about our rule of Platinum Shores. This is about protecting me as his mate. His future wife and hopefully the mother of his children.

Andrew accepts my decision and presses his palm to the small of my back, forcing my feet to move even though my muscles would prefer to stand frozen. It almost feels as if I watch from outside of my body, my curiosity overwhelming to discover what happens next. To see what kind of trouble we face.

Pushing me along, Andrew guides me to the elevator that will take us deeper into the yacht and into the cabins where the rest of the omegas now hide. I'm thankful that he let me be the one to decide whether or not I was going to obey Beckett instead of forcing me into doing what I'm told. It shows how much Andrew respects me as not only his client but also his leader. His boss.

"I want to check on the others," I say, waiting for Andrew to exit the elevator first to check our surroundings.

"I must advise you to reconsider. If the intruders get in, it is best if we're separated." Andrew nudges me to keep walking, following the hallway of wooden doors to the guest cabins on each side. At the end of the hall lies the captain's suite and my personal quarters.

I want to ask him why he feels that it's better to stay away from the omegas, because I know he wouldn't advise it just to do so. He's a bodyguard. He's excellent at strategy and safety.

"Will you check on them, then? Once you know I'm protected?" I don't resist his directions, keeping up his pace and staying at his side.

"I can't make any promises until I assess the situation better. You're my biggest priority, Holly." Hearing my name on his lips sends a shiver through me. Most people would call me by my title. They wouldn't dare say my name, even with my permission, which Andrew does.

And I love that Andrew says it. It's a strange thing to think about in this moment. I should be terrified. I should be rushing to hide, not knowing what kind of enemy we face. Instead, I'm now ultra-aware of how close he is to me. How sweet his scent smells with every inch of his movement.

I don't respond and keep my gaze focused on the world in front of us. I shouldn't be so attracted to this man.

Andrew slows when we reach the last door in the hallway, and he cracks it open to take a peek. Swiveling, I glance behind us, hearing the soft murmur of voices. I hope the omegas aren't scared. I hope Jordan manages to keep them calm. I hope this is all over soon.

"It looks clear," Andrew says, widening the door. "Let me search around really quick. Stay right here." He points at the wall next to the door. "I don't want you in the hallway alone."

Again, I don't argue and instead plant my back against the wall, keeping my hand on my weapon.

Andrew strolls into the suite and opens the tall, narrow closet first, aiming his gun at the emptiness. Making his way to the curtain, covering the door leading to a balcony, he quickly eases it open to look at the dark ocean. It would be difficult but not impossible for someone to reach this balcony.

Striding toward the private bathroom, Andrew swings open the door and points his gun.

A woman screams, startling me, and I step forward raising one of my hands.

"Andrew, that's—"

A gunshot cuts off my words, and I stumble back and hit the wall. Andrew topples backward, landing on the floor.

I stare at the familiar omega leaving the bathroom with a man behind her. A man I had hoped to never see again.

"Hello, Holly." Hector smiles at me, keeping his gun trained on me.

I don't scream.

I don't move.

My vision shadows with an unwanted memory. This is the

leader of Righteous Waters. He was the one accused of my murder.

He's the one who's going to make me pay.

Worthless

BECKETT

I'm a worthless alpha. It's as if the universe wants to show me time and time again that I have no business trying to rule a territory. Yes, Holly is the leader of Platinum Shores, but I'm supposed to be more than her protector and advisor; I'm supposed to be a worthy alpha who ensures our home and territory thrives and doesn't fall by the hands of our enemies.

And we have a lot.

So many that I don't trust anyone outside of my pack and the Gilded Sands Pack. All of these supposed alphas? They're not on my side.

I've never been so overwhelmed in my life.

I wanted Holly to have the best, but with every obstacle, I have come to realize that it might not be me who she needs. And I hate myself for it. I'm so madly in love with her. I will never know a soul like I do hers. She has given me the greatest gift of all, which is her time, love, and affection. She gave me her body. She has truly made me an alpha. If only I could be the one.

A gunshot rings through the air, coming from somewhere within the yacht. I spin around and meet Wesley's gaze, fear stabbing into both of us.

"No one gets in," I say, pointing my gun at Vic. "Prove what kind of leader you are."

Without another word, I race toward the spiral stairwell and jog down two steps at a time, my anxiety screaming that something's wrong. The intruders aren't just on the sundeck or in a boat on the sea beside us. They're already on board and inside. How could I have missed it? We have so much security. Nothing alerted us on the video feeds.

Where have we gone wrong?

"I'm sorry, Holly! I didn't believe you would be successful. I had to take care of myself. Hector promised me a better life. He promised me money and everything I could want without having to give anything in return to an alpha." The feminine voice shrieks the words, the omega talking about someone I'm all too familiar with.

I have studied Hector's criminal record and past. I know he was the leader of Righteous Waters, and one of the top criminals in all of Calico Proper before his territory was dismantled and divided among their Pack Regimes. The only reason he didn't get a death sentence was because the former king of Gilded Sands wanted him to suffer. He wanted him to know what kind of man he had fucked with by murdering his daughter before they even had a chance to make the alliance official.

Neither of them knew that it was all part of an escape plan to get Holly to safety and away from Hector and the rest of Righteous Waters.

And like a wronged ghost, Hector is back to haunt us with a vengeance. Someone in Calico Proper's Pack Regimes was responsible for letting him out of prison without even informing Saint Vista or us.

However wrong it was for the Righteous Waters Pack to be punished for a crime they didn't commit, it's unfathomable that someone thought it right to release them without properly informing their possible victim. They weren't set up without a good reason. They have a violent history that was included in their imprisonment. They're not innocent.

But neither are we.

"Please, Holly. Just go with him. He said he would protect us, and this ensures it. You're our leader. This is your duty," the omega continues, trying to justify what she's done.

It all comes to light, the revelation pissing me off. We have done nothing but try our best to help her. We were going to go through an extravagant plan to ensure that she is never hunted down by the alpha who mistreated her, and here she is, betraying our trust.

Claiming that because Holly is an omega, and because she is the leader of Platinum Shores, that she should be a martyr? Fuck that.

I won't allow it.

My worth might be shaken, but I'll destroy the world for Holly. I didn't want to bring this kind of destruction yet what choice do I have?

"How could you? You should've trusted me," Holly says, her voice remaining even.

"Don't answer her." Hector's gruff voice strikes me in the gut, winding me. "Get to the balcony. I'm not waiting around for this bitch's forgiveness."

I tiptoe closer, saying a silent prayer to the universe that he doesn't hear me. I stay out of sight, walking along the wall. I see a pair of legs on the floor, and I recognize Andrew's boots.

Fuck.

I was hoping for a hostage situation, and not for Holly's bodyguard to be a victim. I was assured he was one of the best and most highly trained alphas in Gilded Sands. He was part of the royal guard.

He didn't even survive a few weeks.

I was hoping he'd be worthy of joining my pack because I need more than just myself as alpha. Holly needs more than just me, and I completely recognize it.

It's one of the reasons why I was so adamant that she picked someone she enjoys the scent of. It's why I wanted her to meet and decide for herself.

Is it weird? Maybe. I admit I was incredibly jealous the moment he was within her reach, accepting his position as her new bodyguard, but I'm over it now.

I feel bad, seeing his lifeless body—

"Holly, duck," Andrew says, his voice surprising me. I can't see him completely, but his legs move and a gun fires. "Run!"

I don't have a chance to brace myself as Holly runs into the hallway, her eyes red with unshed tears. Her mouth drops open at the sight of me, and I hold a finger to my lips, locking my arm around her waist to drag her further away from the captain's suite. Andrew was faking it. Smart man. He probably took a bullet to his vest and not his head. We all wear protection. Especially when we're out and away from the palace.

"I was set up. Hector somehow got to one of the omegas. She arranged this. She didn't believe we could handle the situation," Holly murmurs, her voice shaking.

I growl, anger rushing through me. It's bad enough that alphas underestimate us, but an omega? We have proven to be able to protect them. And one has gone against Holly? After everything?

This is so fucked up.

A part of me wants to run back to the captain's suite and show the omega what happens when you betray the woman of my dreams. Another part of me knows that it's wrong. She did what she believed was right, taking the selfish route. It's her way of taking power back, because she hasn't ever had it. I know Holly wouldn't truly blame the omega either. She's not the type. People are put in hard positions and have to make impossible decisions. We have all been there.

Especially Holly.

Pulling her into one of the cabins, I lock and barricade the door, hoping to get a moment to think and strategize.

"There's no exit here," Holly says, spinning around to search the room. "We have to keep moving."

"We need to stay put until I can think things through." I rub the back of my neck, wishing I could get a better view of the ocean. It's too dark to see anything through the tiny porthole. Things might be different if it were daytime. Unfortunately, I thought it best to use the cover of night to ensure no one tried to intervene when we capsized the boat.

A thought hits me, and I twist and look at Holly. "I think we need to proceed with sinking the vessel. We have our emergency plan in place. We just have to get the omegas to the lifeboat. It's still in the garage."

"Do you think it's safe? What about Hector's pack?" Holly remains close, her hands fisting the fabric of my dress shirt. Her closeness engulfs me with her perfumed skin, her scent awakening every cell on my body.

I tighten my hands into fists. Now's not the time for my fucking body to react this way. I shouldn't want to bend her over and give her my knot as the world burns around us.

I'm assuming more people are on board. If we sink the yacht, we might be able to send them down with it. They're not the only ones capable of seizing a vessel.

Holly frowns, her brows puckering on her forehead. She pushes her blond hair behind her ear, clearing the strands from her face. I wish she didn't have to make these sorts of decisions. We've already risked so much. Anything could go wrong. The omega could've already told Hector about our plan. They could have more men than we do. Stronger weapons. Greater skills. They were a strong enough pack to get the former king, Holly's father, to agree to a union between their families.

But their desire doesn't compare to mine. They want revenge. I want a future with Holly even more.

Her silence speaks volumes, and she gives me the greatest gift of all. Her trust. Her respect and her power. She leaves me in control to handle everything. I might doubt my worth, but I won't stop trying to prove it.

I touch my ear, activating my communication device. "What's your status, Isaiah?"

Tapping my fingers against my hip, I lock my gaze on Holly's as I wait for a response. I shift my attention and stare at the seconds ticking by on my watch, impatiently waiting. It's taking too long.

"Wesley, come in. I need an update." I release the button on my phone device and once again wait, the anticipation bunching my muscles. I haven't heard much commotion. I don't even know what's happening in the captain's suite and if Andrew handled the situation. Each passing second feels like a minute. And a minute feels like an hour.

Again, no one responds to me.

I wrap my hand around Holly's, pulling her close. The last thing I want to do is to stay in this cabin, hoping for the best.

I know Holly grows anxious standing here and waiting. She's active. She has to do something to keep her thoughts at bay. She hasn't been one to just sit around and do nothing. She's the type that if someone else struggles to handle something, she will get up and do it herself. It's one of the things I love about her. She might be an omega, but it doesn't stop her from getting shit done. She learned that from her brothers. It's why the alphas of our territory struggle so much. They're used to omegas being docile. They're used to them always needing something.

That's not my Holly.

"We're going to find the omegas. Jordan should be with them." The moment the comment comes out of my mouth, I start second-guessing myself. Because one of the omegas was in the captain's suite. What if that means something? What if Jordan is hurt or worse?

My heart sinks to my stomach, the thought of my brother in trouble getting the best of me. I promised my parents that I'd always protect him.

I push the thought away and adjust my gun, preparing to fire if I spot someone unfamiliar in the hallway. Cracking open the door, I peer out, unsure what I will find.

I look to the right, half-expecting to see a massacre in the captain's suite, but the door hangs ajar, and I don't see anyone inside. Where did they go? Did Andrew chase Hector off?

Holly clings to my side, not letting any space get between us, and I step into the hallway, trying my best to listen to the rest of the yacht within earshot.

"Don't shoot," Andrew says, stepping from the stairwell next to the elevator. "It's just me."

Holly gasps and yanks away from me, running to Andrew. Stretching up, she cups his face and pats her way down to his chest, stopping where the bullet sunk into his bulletproof vest. He doesn't move or stop her, remaining firm in place as she inspects him for other possible injuries. Any other alpha would be jealous. They'd yank Holly back and scold her for daring to put her hands on another—especially one who isn't a part of our pack, but all I feel is relief. He's alive and still capable of doing his job. He can help me with all the bullshit.

"I thought it went through. I thought you died," Holly whispers, her voice like a breath of air settling my nerves.

"I would've, had I not played dead. I'm sorry for scaring you. It was my way of keeping you safe. I knew the bastard wouldn't attempt to kill you." Andrew slowly lifts his hand and covers Holly's as it rests on his shoulder. His eyes flick to mine, and I remain expressionless. I'm not going to react either way. I might have claimed Holly with my knot, but she's still a free woman until we make things official. She might not think that way, but I do. I can't help it. I was raised to believe that I'd never have an omega as just my own. I always knew I would share if I ever had the chance. At least, if she was willing. And Holly is.

"He would've had to kill me because there's no way I would've left this yacht willingly." Holly shivers, and I step even closer, lacing my hands around her waist until she catches my scent and leans back, pressing her back to my chest. I want her to know that I'm here. Physically and emotionally. And knowing that she would rather die than be taken by Righteous Waters... I don't know how that makes me feel. If she were taken, I'd still have hope. I'd have a reason to live. But if she were—no. I can't think about it.

"Neither of those situations would've happened. Not on my watch," Andrew says, his muscles flexing in his arms, his fingers still curled around Holly's as I envelop her from behind.

"Or on mine. Hector knows this. He just wants to torment you while he can." I bury my face into the crook of her neck and kiss her soft skin, wanting nothing more than to spin her around.

I don't have to yearn for long, because she does, twisting to face me. Snaking her hands around my neck, she pulls me in close and kisses me, giving me the affection I so desperately crave.

"I want him to sink with this yacht," Holly says. The low

growl to her voice surprises me, the rumble sexy.

I open my mouth to agree with her, but an alarm blares. The noise is loud enough to steal my hearing. It's the fire alarm. Sprinklers activate and spray, sending water pelting over our bodies.

I inhale a deep breath, trying to catch the scent of the invisible smoke, but all I can pick up is Holly's fragrance. Andrew's too.

Something bangs, smacking the stairs. I push Holly against Andrew and spin around. Lifting my gun, I aim, blinking my eyes to clear water from my lashes.

Some sort of can smacks the bottom of the spiral staircase next to the elevator, golden liquid pouring out and mixing with the water from above.

The sprinklers suddenly cut off.

A strange crackle soon follows.

"Run! Head to the captain's suite!" I yell, scrambling back, bumping into Holly and Andrew.

Flames burst across the floor.

The yacht is set ablaze.

11

Bitter Revenge

HOLLY

Death by fire is a death I don't want. It's the death that my brothers had helped me fake, and I'm afraid it might become a reality now. Bitter revenge for the Righteous Waters Pack. They want to take me out the same way they were accused of killing me. But this time, there are far too many lives at stake.

I have failed my pack. I have failed the omegas in my territory. But worst of all, I have failed myself.

"We're going to have to jump. Grab the life jackets. If we

can move quickly enough, we might be able to secure one of the lifeboats. Maybe a jet ski." Beckett instructs Andrew who grabs three life vests from the closet.

"We should board their boat. It's probably our safest bet. If we can take it over, we can save the others." Andrew absently helps me into my life vest and buckles it before sliding on his own. Beckett clicks his in place and grabs a few of the couch cushions and throws them off the balcony. Andrew rushes back and grabs the remaining ones for us, tossing them out into the ocean, following Beckett's lead.

They still manage to think of others even as our lives face unimaginable danger.

I cough and turn away from the fire creeping across the walls and door of the captain's suite. The yacht sways and creaking noises come from nowhere and everywhere. I try to ignore people yelling. Screaming. This vessel will burn before it sinks.

"I need to contact my packmates. They haven't responded to my calls." Beckett bounces on his feet, watching the flames draw closer and closer.

"We'll find them," I say, speaking up for what feels like the first time. "We need to get off the yacht first. The fire's intense. I don't know how much longer I can handle standing here."

Beckett tightens his jaw and looks at Andrew. "Are you a good swimmer?"

He nods.

"Then you go first. Catch Holly. Don't let her go under the boat." Beckett curls and uncurls his fingers, his face set aglow with the hot fire now halfway across the suite, the blaze intense and crackling because of the gasoline someone threw down the stairs. They really wanted to make sure this place went up in flames. Even the sprinkler system couldn't keep up with it.

Andrew touches my shoulder, getting me to look at him. "I need you to jump as far away as you can from the boat. I don't want you to get caught in the current, okay? As soon as you hit the water, I'll grab you. We're going to swim as far as we can as quickly as we can. Got it?"

All I can do is squeak out my agreement. I don't have long legs like he does, but at least I can swim.

"If we get separated, get her back to shore. Do not put her in the middle of a fight despite what she says." Beckett doesn't look at me as he says the words. He and Andrew have a silent conversation right in front of me.

I don't get the chance to argue, because he motions for Andrew to go, and my bodyguard leaps off the balcony, jumping down several levels and into the ocean.

Beckett kisses me, molding his lips to mine, the desperation coursing from him giving me a bad feeling. This isn't the type of kiss I want. This is a kiss that feels as if it might be goodbye.

"Beck—"

"Jump, Holly!" Beckett commands, thrusting his hand out. "Jump!"

My body takes control, shoving my mind away. and I automatically leap from the balcony, closing my eyes as the world rushes around me. Wind tingles through my hair, and the ocean roars in my ear before I break the surface, sinking under several feet into pitch darkness. The water steals my hearing. It's as if I've been transported into a void, and it plans to swallow me whole.

I kick my legs, praying that I'm headed in the right direction, because the life vest doesn't drag me quick enough to the surface, the ocean stronger than I realized. What if I didn't jump far enough out? What if I'm being yanked under the boat?

Panic spins through my mind, and I jerk around, running out of air. I thought dying in a fire would be awful, but drowning? This is just as bad. My lungs burn. Hopelessness courses through me.

I give up fighting the pull of the ocean and let it take me. That's when I break through the surface and gasp a breath of fresh sea air.

"I got you, Holly. Come on, kick your legs. Swim." Andrew tugs me by the back of my life vest, keeping my face toward the sky. I stare up through my blurry vision at the stars, the brilliant universe stretching out into the infinite to beyond.

"Where's Beckett?" I ask, trying my best to stretch my neck to look around. I spot the yacht to my right, the flames eating away at the back of the boat. It hasn't worked its way toward the front yet.

People gather on the bow, and some float in the water.

"Keep swimming," Andrew instructs, not answering my question. It's as if he's avoiding answering. Beckett should've been right behind me.

It's enough to make me stop kicking and pull away from Andrew. His fingers slip off my life jacket, and I spin around and search the choppy waters.

"Holly, we need to keep going. The Righteous Waters Pack is too busy watching their destruction. Beckett can handle himself. He knows what he's doing. We need to get on that boat. It might be our only chance." Andrew draws my attention away from the chaos and toward the old fishing boat, bobbing on the water far enough from the yacht to get a good view but not to get caught up in the chaos.

I'm torn between screaming out for Beckett or following Andrew. He might be right. We can swim to the back of the boat, hopefully going unnoticed. Then we can attack.

His plan goes against Beckett's orders. Beckett wants me away from the fight. But this is my fight. The Righteous Waters

Pack is here because of me. They won't stop until they either win or I take them out. There's no other way.

So I inhale a deep breath and swim, taking control of my movements and staying beside Andrew.

My body aches, and my breath comes in heavy pants, the exertion making it hard to keep going. Twenty feet. Ten feet. I expect someone to start shooting at us. I expect Hector to be waiting. For him to yank me out of the water to toss me on the dirty deck.

Luckily, it's empty.

"Killing me won't give you power!" Beckett's familiar voice cuts through the air, shocking me to my core. I don't understand. Where is he? "But working together will. You can't fault me for the position I accepted. You know that a pack like mine would never have been offered such power otherwise."

Furrowing my brows, I hang on to the back of the boat, the swimming ladder icy under my touch from the cold air.

I shift my gaze to Andrew in confusion. "What the—"

He presses his hand to my mouth, silencing my voice.

"I don't know why you brought him aboard, Hector. You should have taken the jet ski and let him drown. Just shoot him and get it over with. We can steal our power back by force," another guy says, his voice unfamiliar.

"You won't. You're not as powerful as you once were. But

Holly is my omega. I can persuade her. I can put her in her place. Don't kill me and hear me out," Beckett says, his words like a slap in the face.

I don't understand what's going on. Beckett got to a jet ski? He didn't choose to save us and instead came here alone? Is this why he demanded Andrew keep me out of a supposed fight?

Andrew climbs up the rungs and pulls me from the water, pressing his index finger over his mouth, silently begging me to be quiet. He searches around the deck, finding a net. I grab a broom, holding it like it could protect me in a gunfight. I know it won't, but I don't know what else to do. I lost my weapon along the way. I don't see another one here. I'm not strong, but I'm an excellent fighter. My brothers made sure.

"Do you think I trust you to follow through? I need a guarantee before I negotiate anything." Hector's familiar voice sends goosebumps over my skin. I can't believe Beckett is even here. He had this planned since the fire started, which is why he sent me with Andrew.

But I don't feel as if he's betrayed me. I'm just in shock. Hurt. I think he's desperate. Beckett has struggled for months with proving he is capable of running a territory. But resorting to this? God, no. My sweet, protective alpha. What has this done to him?

"I have given you no reason to trust me, so no. What kind

of guarantee? Property? A leadership position on one of the bigger packs?" Beckett remains even in tone, sounding as if this is just a part of his everyday life.

"I want the omegas. I also want restitution for the time I lost. For the packmates I lost. You killed my brother," Hector says, his voice deep with anger.

I tense, jerking my attention away from Andrew. He doesn't give away a single thought. All he does is adjust the net between his hands and tilt his head to the side, motioning to a metal ladder that goes up to the helm of the boat.

"He knows what he's doing," Andrew whispers, knowing that if he doesn't say something soon, I might lose my shit. It takes everything in me not to rush around the pathway to the bow of the boat.

"He's not the leader of Platinum Shores. He can't make these offerings," I mutter, hating that it has come to this.

"They don't know that. They don't know anything. Now, come on. We must attack from above. We're running out of time." Andrew gets me to step on the first rung, trusting me to go first. He waits until I make it to the top. I set the broom against the metal wall and peer into the console, spotting a man sitting in front of the navigation equipment. He focuses on his screen, not even looking up.

From here, I can't hear Beckett any longer. It makes me want to hurry.

I don't wait for Andrew to finish scaling the ladder before I yank open the door of the console and slam the broom handle to the top of the guy's head. It's enough to stun him but he doesn't go down.

I search around, spotting his weapon on his hip. I crouch and grab it, yanking it free while shoving my arm against his chair, not letting him turn around.

He hollers, his voice echoing, and I cringe and slap the side of his head with the barrel of the gun. If I shoot him, it will draw even more attention.

But I don't have to. Andrew looms over me and grabs the guy by his head, twisting hard and sharp, breaking his neck and cutting off all his noise.

The man slips down and Andrew flexes his jaw with a hard look at me.

"Can you drive a boat?" Andrew asks, turning the captain's chair around.

I shake my head. "I can shoot a gun. I will not let Beckett make this mistake. You can either stay here and wait for my instructions or you can follow me."

"Holly—"

"No. There is only one way to handle this, and it's not by negotiation. We don't negotiate with people who'll turn around and stab us in the back." I straighten my shoulders and check the gun, ensuring that the clip is loaded.

Andrew grabs a fishing knife from its spot stuck into the wood panel of the wall, and he swipes it on his wet jeans.

I knew he wouldn't stay here, defending the cockpit. He is my bodyguard, and I know he won't leave my side.

"Becks? What the fuck?" Jordan's voice rings through the air, his surprise turning it higher in pitch. "Where's Holly?"

I move faster, my heart feeling like a rock in my chest, smashing against my rib cage with every beat.

"She's none of your concern. She's safe, and that's all that matters. We have bigger things to deal with besides a disobedient omega." Beckett lowers his voice, his words dripping with what feels like anger. But it's not directed toward anyone. He's mad at himself. I know him well enough to notice. He hates saying things that he knows will hurt his brother.

"What the fuck?" Jordan repeats. "You are—"

Jordan's voice cuts off, and he grunts, pain radiating with his groan.

I duck beside Andrew and look over the railing, spotting the group on the deck of the boat. Some men keep their backs away from Hector and another guy looming over my mates, watching as our yacht capsizes. The roar of the ocean and the sound of destruction is too loud to hear the people in the water.

My fear prevents me from even glancing in that direction. What if my packmates are out there? What if they're not? I still have no idea where Wesley and Isaiah are. Because I don't think they're here.

"Don't talk to an alpha like that, you bastard beta." Hector snarls with the words. He shakes out his hand, his knuckles bloody, but it doesn't compare to Jordan's bruised face.

Jordan scowls at Hector, but he keeps his mouth shut.

"There are only two ways this will go. You will give me restitution for the loss of my brother, and you'll bow and give me your pack name, so I can take back what is mine, or you can close your eyes and die." Hector aims the gun at Beckett. "Your omega is mine. All of them are mine. Make your choice. I will get what I want regardless."

Andrew flares his nostrils, spreading his arms wider with the net.

"I'm not dying," Beckett says, keeping his back straight.

Hector turns the gun toward Jordan. "Good. A brother for a brother."

It's as if the world stops. I can't breathe. I can't think. All I can do is watch as Hector slides his finger over the trigger.

I smash my finger to my own trigger, firing the weapon I stole from the dead man. The bullet hits the deck, missing

Hector by a foot. I wasn't focused enough. My hands are far too shaky.

And now it has drawn attention to me.

Andrew flings the net, sending it cascading over the deck and onto the guys. Jordan takes advantage of the distraction and rams his shoulders into Hector's gut, sending him toppling over.

Swinging his legs over the railing, Andrew jumps the twelve feet from above and lands on top of another alpha. He stabs him through the back of the neck, killing him immediately.

All I can do is stand and watch the fight unfold, aiming my gun but not shooting. I can't tell who is who, the arms flailing, the bodies rolling. The fists flying.

I've never seen so much blood in my life. I can't tell who it comes from or if it's fatal. And then I spot Hector cutting his way out of the net.

"He's getting away!" I shout, pointing at the alpha, grabbing Andrew's attention.

But I can't get to the man in time. Hector passes something over the side of the boat and dives into the water. A few others follow his lead, choosing to flee, knowing that if they continue to fight, they'll die. Even though my pack is split up, with Andrew by their sides, Beckett and Jordan manage to overpower Righteous Waters. They manage to work together quickly and efficiently as if it were meant to be.

A small motor steals my attention, and I rush to the side of the boat and peer down, watching as an inflatable motorboat comes to life. I can't let Hector get away. If he gets away, I won't have time to strategize.

He'll come back even harder. More vile. And who knows what would happen.

I aim my gun, steadying my hands. I can't be shaky. Not now.

Hector meets my gaze and smiles, yanking a body in front of him. He pulls off a bag from Bonnie's head, the omega who betrayed me screaming out.

I spot two other women in the getaway boat and wonder where the rest of them are. They might still be on board. These assholes decided to take what they could and leave.

Now I'm afraid for these women's fates.

I redirect my aim and shoot at the motor, hoping to blow it up. It pelts off the metal box and disappears into the night. I adjust my target, pulling the trigger, but nothing happens. The clip is empty.

Hector steers the motorboat, driving it away, leaving me on the fishing boat. I stare at the burning yacht, wondering what the hell my life has come to.

How will we recover from this? How will we explain it?

I pray that the Pack Regimes don't turn against us and consider me unfit for this territory. I'll lose everything.

I might even lose myself.

12

A Pack's Strength

HOLLY

"Relax, my queen. You've been through a lot. It's okay to take a breath." Jordan kneels on the floor in front of me, resting his hands on my knees.

"Not until we have those omegas back. I can't just sit around and wait." I fall back to the bed, sprawling out and staring at the ceiling.

"We will do everything we can as quickly as we can. Beckett has put in a call to an ally in Calico Proper. They're going to check the security from the region's prison." Wesley stands in the doorway to Jordan's suite, and I spot Isaiah behind him. I don't have to see Andrew to know he keeps out of the way, guarding the hallway. I can smell him from here, his scent stronger than my loving betas.

"Where is Beckett?" I ask, resting on my elbows.

"He needed to do some things. We are in charge of you now, lovely." Wesley strolls forward, his eyes roving over my body. "I'm starving for your affection. Last night was one of the hardest in my life. All I could think about was how I was stranded in the water and unable to find you."

Because Wesley and Isaiah had to jump off the yacht as it burned, remaining with the alpha leaders of our territory. We found them immediately after Hector left, and it was for the best not to follow them and risk losing more lives.

Because they had help from one of the omegas, the Righteous Waters pack managed to sneak onto the yacht and overpower Jordan. They were already off the boat before the fire started. He was taken with them, beat up and bound until Beckett arrived. Beckett still hasn't told me anything. Neither has Jordan. It's as if they have promised each other not to speak a word about what really happened apart from what I've heard about Beckett trying to negotiate with Hector. It wasn't to betray me—that I'm sure of—but risking Jordan? I don't know how I feel. I don't want to think about it anymore. I just want to move on with our lives.

"Will you give me a moment of your time?" Wesley asks, sitting on the edge of the bed. He rests his hand on my leg, his warm fingers still managing to stir goosebumps across my body.

"And will you allow me to give you a moment of mine?" Isaiah plops down on my other side, sandwiching me between him and Wesley. Jordan remains on the floor, kneeling between my legs, his expression eager, the lust prevalent as I inhale a deep breath. My betas might not have strong scents like my alpha, but I can still read them like my personal journal. They crave me. They want nothing more than to help me forget.

I should feel badly wanting to give in, because I was unable to protect those omegas. Except right now, there isn't much I can do. I'm not all-powerful. I might have been given this leadership position, but there's a lot more to it than flexing power. I need to work on my alliances. I need to really prove that I'm capable, and stuff like that takes time. It takes intelligence and strategizing. I can't just run around all of the territories, guns blazing, demanding justice and revenge.

"I don't know if I'm able to give you my full attention," I murmur, pressing my back harder to the mattress. "I have a lot on my mind."

"That's a challenge I'm willing to accept. Do you know how

jealous I am that Jordan has managed to sweep you off your feet? I always expected it would be Beckett first. I would've done things differently had I known." Wesley leans on his elbow, lying down beside me. He draws his finger across my temple, combing my pale blond hair behind my ear. "Will you let me make up for it? For my shortcomings? For my inability to realize that you're not only Beckett's omega. You're mine."

I shiver, his warm breath tickling my ear as he sucks my earlobe into his mouth. I have kissed Wesley a dozen times in the last few weeks since Beckett claimed me. I've slept in his bed and explored his body. And he's explored mine, but we've never gone beyond that. As for the thought now? I want to know what he feels like. I want to know what it's like to be loved by my three betas in intimate ways.

"What if I told you that you're not the only one who has been starved for affection? You three have been so amazing to me. I thought I'd made it clear that I want the bond of a pack, not just an alpha." My words come out as a purr, my voice sultry. My body now hums at the growing desire permeating the air.

"I love you, Holls," Isaiah says, drawing his thumb across my chin, getting me to turn my head away from Wesley. He guides me closer, pressing his lips to mine, kissing me sensually, sweetly, his affection as addicting as his closeness.

"I love you, Isaiah. I just want things to settle down so I can constantly show you just how much." I suck his bottom lip between my teeth, nipping him gently, pulling a growl from his mouth.

The sensation rumbles through me, awakening every molecule in my body. This is exactly what I needed after last night. I had no idea as much, yet a part of me is still missing. I'm afraid that Beckett might pull away because of everything. It's a lot of stress and the heaviest burden to carry, being the sole alpha of a pack, especially one in a position such as ours.

"While they're loving up on you, I just want to taste your sweet pussy, my queen. It's been days." Jordan groans and kisses my knee, his boldness always getting to me in a good way. He speaks like an alpha, while Isaiah and Wesley tread more lightly.

I laugh in exasperation, licking my lips as I peek at him between my legs, already grabbing at my panties to pull them down. I squirm and lean back completely, clutching onto both Isaiah and Wesley as Jordan drags me toward the edge of the bed, dangling my legs off for better reach.

"You just have to tell her what you want to do," Jordan says, mumbling as he works his mouth over my thigh. "You know she gets tired of always having to make decisions. Tell her what you want."

I moan and squirm, Jordan finally burying his face to the apex of my legs, dragging his tongue over my clit to suck it gently into his mouth, the sensation enough to make me dig my fingers into Wesley's leg.

"I want to undress you," Wesley says, sliding his fingers under the soft fabric of my shirt, tracing over my skin.

"Is that okay?" Isaiah caresses his fingers over my breast, feeling my hardening nipple. I don't wear a bra underneath my nightshirt, barely long enough to cover my body, not that Jordan allows such an obstruction of view from my betas. "I want to give you what you crave. You said you wanted a pack bond. Can we give that to you?"

I arch my back and squeeze Jordan between my thighs, the consistent licking of his tongue enough to bring me to my peak. I scream out in pleasure, unable to answer Isaiah. But I don't need to.

I just give in and roll on top of him, dragging my fingers across his pants, rushing to unbuckle his belt.

"Damn, my queen. Seeing your ass like that—" A warm hand smacks my butt cheek, sending a wave of heated pleasure right to my clit. "Let me fuck you while you fuck him. I can see you've already taken control from Isaiah."

"He's mine," I say, squirming on top of him. "You're all mine."

Lust clouds my mind, and I don't stop until I pull out Isaiah's cock and align it to my body, sinking down completely. He digs his fingers into my hips, his eyes locked to mine. I rock my body hard and fast, just wanting to keep my focus on my guys. On the pleasure they arouse in me.

"She's so hot," Wesley says, kneeling close by, grabbing my head to kiss me as I ride Isaiah.

"I want to taste you," I gasp, reaching for his pants. He doesn't let me and does it himself, shrugging free of his clothing.

Jordan kisses my shoulders and squeezes my ass, working his hands up to my back until he guides me forward to bow on top of Isaiah, my body refusing to stop my rocking movements, the pleasure making me moan over and over again.

Grabbing my hips, Jordan slows my body, and I whimper, my need getting more intense. I just want my betas to fill me up in a way I have never experienced. I want them to show exactly what it's like to be loved by a pack.

"You're so wet," Jordan murmurs.

I moan as he slides his cock into my pussy with Isaiah's, stretching me in a way that leaves me shaking. He doesn't stay inside me for long, shifting slightly as he aligns his hips to my ass, wanting to fuck me from behind, my slick lubricating me so much I know it'll fill me with pleasure and not pain. I'm strong enough for anything.

"God, that's so sexy," Wesley says, rubbing his fingers along my back. "You want Jordan, don't you?"

I whimper in agreement, my breath heavy, my voice refusing to speak my words.

Jordan eases his cock between my ass cheeks, my slick drenching all of us, bringing me pure satisfaction as he fills me in a way my body is made for. I bite my teeth into Isaiah's pec, leaving my mark as the two of them find their rhythm, working together to fuck me like I crave.

Wesley grabs my chin and tilts my head up, aligning his cock with my mouth. I stick out my tongue and drag it across his shaft before sucking his tip in, letting him sink into my throat, my mouth watering to taste his cum.

To be loved by a pack is an honor and a blessing I never expected. They don't use me for their pleasure. We are together in love, bonding in a way that will make us stronger. That'll make us fight harder.

It's a bond that will never be broken.

Wesley pumps into my mouth, and I hum, feeling his cock pulse as he comes, the flavor tangy like his scent. He pulls out and slides his hand over my breasts, pinching my nipples and working his way down until he slides his finger over my clit, not even caring how close he is to Isaiah's cock. He rubs until

I reach my peak again, my orgasm so intense that I clutch onto Isaiah and Jordan with my body, slowing them down, the sensation enough to set them off. Heat fills me up, and I gasp and lie forward, feeling Isaiah's heart pounding against mine. Jordan rests on top of me with Wesley beside me, the three of them like a protective wall of muscle. A wall of love.

They mean so much to me in this moment that I could fall asleep and continue to forget the world outside of us. So that's what I do.

I lose myself to the utter bliss they awaken inside me. I lose myself to what life should be like.

If only it could always be this perfect.

13

Pack Bonds

HOLLY

Beckett stands at his desk, his back facing me as he presses his phone to his ear. His rigid muscles flex, and he keeps his voice low. I haven't seen him in a whole day, and I can't stand it any longer. I understand he's trying to locate the Righteous Waters Pack, but I'm starting to feel as if he's pulling away to do things on his own.

"I'm in over my head," Beckett says, his voice swirling to me. "You should've seen the look on her face, Wilder. It broke my heart. I didn't know what else to do though. I don't know if

I'm really cut out for this."

"Don't start doubting yourself. You know the expectation. You must remain as her counsel if you want to marry her. She is a leader of the Pack Regimes, and with that comes a lot of bullshit. I don't like it half the time, but we can manage. You can manage. I've seen you work your ass off. You're already building a great relationship with the other leaders. If you don't think you can handle this, then you need to figure shit out." Wilder's voice booms through the air, loud with the speakerphone.

It makes me hesitate, and I stop in my place and eavesdrop, wanting to know exactly what's going on with Beckett.

"I'm just afraid of letting her down. I'm not going any-where, Wilder. She is the one I want, even if this position ends up killing me. It would be better than a life without her. You know we are dying to make it official. The Pack Regimes need to agree already." Beckett scrubs the back of his neck, shifting on his feet. He spots me in his peripheral vision and frowns.

I tip my head to the side, his comment surprising me. "What do you mean the Pack Regimes need to agree?" I stride for-ward, my muscles tensing.

"Holly, calm down before you start lashing out. You know I'm not going to speak to you if you're going to act like my annoying little sister," Wilder snaps, his command reminding me that even though he's not my alpha, he's still one, and he can get under my skin.

"I *am* your annoying little sister. So what the fuck did I just hear? Explain it, and you better not say that the leaders need to approve of my marriage. I have been waiting for Beckett to ask me. And now that I know why he hasn't? What the actual hell, Wilder?" I stand with my hands on my hips even though he can't see me through the line. I know he can envision me though. We've had enough arguments to know what to expect from each other.

Wilder puffs out of breath, causing static in the line. "They're not preventing you from marriage. However, they have to unanimously agree that the Silversteins can handle being on your pack. You should know by now that things have always been a little complicated when it comes to who rules the territories. They're humoring us because Platinum Shores was given to Gilded Sands, and we gave it to you. The last thing the leaders want is for another war to break out. This is why the Silversteins must show they're capable of standing beside you to rule. You know it's harder when there's only one alpha." Wilder remains calm with his words, so they piss me off, and it takes everything in me not to start screaming.

Because what was the point of giving me a territory if I can't have the people I need by my side?

"You better convince them, brother. I have enough to deal with. I will marry the Silversteins. Do you understand?" My chest heaves with my growing anger, though it's not truly directed at Wilder.

"Holly, you need to convince them. Not me. If this is too much for you—"

I snatch the phone from Beckett's hand and hang up on Wilder, my emotions getting the best of me.

Beckett closes the space and envelops me in his arms, pulling me against his chest. He rests his chin on my shoulder and sucks in deep breaths, savoring the scent of my skin and hair. He doesn't speak. He doesn't try to reason with me about the situation with the Pack Regimes. All he does is hold me close, hugging me as if it's all he wants to do.

"Why didn't you tell me?" I ask, my voice a murmur. I wouldn't yell at Beckett for this. I can already sense that he is overwhelmed and second-guessing himself. "We could've figured something out already."

Groaning, he kisses the crook of my neck, holding me tighter. "I didn't think it would be so hard. I was ready to propose to you the moment we moved into this palace. Our pack has been so anxious about it. I didn't want to let you guys down. You would know how worthless I am because the Pack Regimes still hasn't approved of anything."

"Worthless? I would never call you worthless. You have done so much and have proved over and over again that you are capable of being a good alpha to me. You show compassion. You stand down when I need to rise. You help me make the best decisions possible for our people. You're not worthless. You are priceless. The Pack Regimes are stubborn and stupid if they think otherwise. I will not stand for this. I am marrying you. I am marrying the Silverstein Pack. I'm taking your name, and there is nothing, and I mean fucking nothing, anyone can do about it. They can try to take back this territory, but it won't be easy. They'll see. They have spent so long taking and taking without consideration that it's time they realize that the only reason they have been allowed to do such things is because we have let them. The people have let them. Not anymore." My voice grows stronger with each of my words, my convictions hot and ready to be put to the test. It's one thing to question my ability to lead. It's another thing to make my alpha feel as if he isn't worthy of me. And I'm so pissed off for it.

"Holly...I love you. I love you with my entire being, but things are complicated. You have so much faith in me but look at what happened. Look at the position I put you in. I went rogue, wanting nothing more than to put Hector in his place, and he still bested me. I can't do this alone." Beckett keeps his face hidden, his lips brushing against my skin.

Confusion puckers my brow and I try to pull away, but he doesn't let me. He needs me close, touching him. He needs to stay hidden to be able to speak his mind.

I rub my hand over his shoulders. "You're not supposed to do this alone. We're a pack."

"I'm the only alpha." Beckett refuses to look at me.

I crane my neck, sliding my hand under his chin, cupping his jaw, guiding him to look up and meet my gaze. "That's what this is about? Because an alpha doesn't make the pack strong. An alpha helps us lead. An alpha keeps me safe. But an alpha does not give the pack power. It's every single one of us."

"I know that, but no one else sees it that way. Things might be changing, but it's still difficult. You have to have the strongest pack, Holly. I can't keep relying on your brothers. We need to think about what's best for us. I want to proposition Andrew. He has shown himself loyal. He has the skills we need." Beckett's eyes line with tears, but they don't fall. He would never let them fall for me to see.

I blink a few times, trying to wrap my mind around what he says. "You know the difficulties that come with inviting another alpha. There are expectations. The way packs with strong alpha leaders manage is because—"

"Of their omega," Beckett finishes, speaking my thoughts out loud for me.

"I don't know…" I have never truly thought of strengthening our pack by bringing in another. Usually packs grow by creating families within them. By extending lifelong friendships and connections. What he's saying would mean entrusting our entire future with someone we have just met weeks ago. Someone we have hired as a bodyguard compared to growing a foundation that takes years and years.

"I've seen your connection for myself. I saw how you reacted to him. How he looks at you. I know this is a huge ask, but will you think about it? We can have specific arrangements. We can work things out if you truly are against this. I just want to be the best I can be for you." Beckett stares into my eyes, his brown irises glittering with his unshed tears. This is probably the hardest thing he's had to admit. The hardest thing to even think about.

He has always been the only alpha in his pack. His sisters, his cousins, everyone he has surrounded himself with is a beta. He's one of the rare to manifest into an alpha, taking over the Silverstein name for his father. That's why the Silverstein Pack has never been in complete control of a territory. They've always just helped the leaders.

"If this is what you feel we need, then I will keep an open mind." I purse my lips, wondering how the hell we're going to bring this up with Andrew. What if he doesn't want anything to do with this? Because if he joins our pack, things will change. How exactly? I have no idea.

"I just want to discuss it with everyone. I think it will help our situation. People will be less likely to constantly plot against us. Andrew comes from an esteemed pack in Gilded Sands. It could really benefit our situation." It sounds as if Beckett has been thinking about this for a while, even longer than just this last day. I should've suspected something when I was to choose the scent I found most desirable. It's as if he was setting me up on a blind date, but more to bring someone into our pack compared to trying to set me up for anything romantic.

"What about our relationship? You're my alpha. You know that the Pack Regimes have expectations. Andrew might not even be on board. He might not even like me. You could be reading everything wrong." I refrain from speaking about how I feel, because I know my attraction and it would be a lie if I said anything otherwise. I've never kept a secret from Beckett. It's one of those things we have yet to explore, our own need to bond with each other still new.

It's funny. My brothers had asked me if this was what I wanted. They were concerned that I was infatuated with the Silversteins because they were the first guys to show me affection. The first guys who treated me like an equal and stood by my side. They thought my naivety would cloud my judgment, because I lacked the experience they thought I needed.

I didn't think I needed experience to know what I wanted.

But now? Maybe I do.

What's the worst that can happen? I've already been through hell. This might be what I need to show that I'm a good ruler. I don't do what is only best for myself. I do what is best for my pack.

I do what is best for our future.

Even if it means a little compromise.

And that's where I've seen others go wrong. They can't adapt to things changing. They prefer things to stay the same.

But not me. I look forward to the change.

I strive for it.

14

Seducing Alphas

HOLLY

I thought I was over my nerves. I still get butterflies in my stomach for my guys, but there's something different about the situation.

"How do you even bring this up?" I ask, sitting on the edge of the couch, bouncing the balls of my feet. "You can't expect me to say, 'hey, big alpha. Want to join my pack? Want to know what it's like to have me as an omega? I'll be a good girl.' This is so crazy." Heat burns my skin with my words, the seriousness of the situation turning me a bit loopy. I would never speak to someone like that. My anxiety makes me feel dumb.

Jordan chuckles and laces his fingers through mine. "That would totally work on me. You are the hottest woman in the world. A perfect ten."

I squeeze my eyes shut and giggle, unable to stop fidgeting. "You're too much."

"You could just seduce him and make him fall so madly in love with you that there is no other option." Wesley rests his hand on my knee, gently squeezing and sending tingles blooming up my thighs. "It worked on me."

Tipping my head back, I laugh out loud, my voice ringing through the air. I expected things to be more difficult than they are, but I guess my betas kind of have been expecting this. They've known Beckett forever. They had their suspicions when he suggested that they hire an alpha bodyguard. I think it was his need to prove his worthiness that really kept him from speaking his mind truthfully.

And it's as if a weight has already been lifted off his shoulders. He smiles softly, for what feels like the first time in over a week.

"How about we start with being honest. This is about our pack as a whole and not Holly alone." Beckett crosses his arms over his chest, straightening his back, looking hot and bossy even if he is only making a suggestion. The others will see it more as a command.

"You say that now but wait until someone else shows off their knot," Isaiah says, his lips quirking in the corners with his smile. "You've never had to deal with another alpha vying for Holly's attention."

Beckett lifts an eyebrow. "I've dealt with dozens. Every fucking alpha in this territory has their eyes on Holly. I know how to handle myself."

"We'll see when it comes to a sword fight," Jordan teases, swinging his hips. He brings my hand to his mouth for a kiss.

If they continue speaking, I might burn up and disintegrate on this couch cushion. I was more in tune with what Beckett imagined. My mind might have suggested that bringing another alpha into our pack would mean more possibilities, but I wasn't going to assume. And my betas automatically think that because Beckett wants to bring Andrew into the pack that it means he will automatically have me.

I should be weirded out by the thought, but all it does is make me giggle and blush. God this is going to be so uncomfortable. We don't even know if Andrew will agree, but my guys act as if there's no other option.

"There will be no fighting. Now I want you guys to keep your mouths shut. Not a single word." Beckett scrubs his hand through his hair, messing up the strands. "You'll be good little betas and let us handle things."

Jordan lifts a finger to his forehead, saluting his brother. "Yes, sir. I won't fuck things up for Holly."

"For us," Beckett corrects, striding toward the door of the office where Andrew waits outside, watching protectively over the palace on my behalf.

My eyes widen, assuming what he plans to do next, the idea kicking my body into action. I hop from my seat and rush, jumping up onto his back.

I thought things would be more subtle, bringing it up more privately instead of in front of all of us. If I were Andrew, I'd run away. That's a lot to take in without having time to process.

Beckett loses his footing and stumbles forward smacking his hands into the door. I fall away and scream, unable to catch myself before I fall on the carpet.

Commotion breaks out as Isaiah swears, getting up from his seat. The door to the office swings open and Andrew appears in the doorway, his eyes narrowed, his muscles flexing as he reaches for his weapon.

His stern features smooth out when he gets a look around, seeing that there is no threat. "My apologies. It sounded like there was an attack."

Beckett pushes up on his knees. "There was."

Andrew tenses again, and Wesley and Isaiah laugh out loud. Jordan gets to his feet and closes the space to me, picking me up from the floor.

"You have to be careful with this one. She will physically try to stop you from doing something she is nervous about." Jordan cradles me like a blushing bride and kisses my temple. "I got her now. Beckett's safe."

Andrew cocks his head, staring at me with a dozen questions in his eyes. He's confused about the entire situation and what my guys are speaking about.

"Oh," Andrew says, slowly backing away toward the office door. "Again, I'm sorry for the interruption. Like I said, I thought—"

"You are a good man," Beckett says, cutting off his second apology. "Never apologize for doing your job. There very well could've been an attack. You've seen how things are."

Andrew relaxes, slowing down his steps so he hovers just inside the open door. "It's unfortunate. Holly doesn't deserve the sort of worry."

Jordan brushes his lips to my ear. "See? He's already sympathetic."

I elbow him, keeping my eyes trained on Andrew. He watches me watch him; our gazes locked on each other. It's how he always is, giving me his complete attention despite the others in the room. It sends goosebumps over my skin, my thoughts now whirling with the ideas my betas put in my mind about another alpha on our pack. It's awkward, but only because I don't know how Andrew will react.

"None of us do," I say softly, hoping if I speak up that the others won't. I wouldn't put it past Jordan to insinuate something. "It has gotten a lot easier though, especially with you around." There. I said something that will hopefully get a reaction.

"It is my honor to protect you," Andrew responds, again keeping his eyes locked on mine.

"That's exactly what we like to hear." Beckett glances from me and to our other packmates. "It's more important than ever. Holly needs extra support during this time, and we're relieved that you're here to give it. Keep up the good work."

What is he doing? The thought scrambles around my mind as Beckett gets to his feet and motions toward the others.

"We have a couple of meetings we need to attend. Would you mind escorting Holly into town, and then we will meet you there? She has arranged a gathering with the Pack Regimes." Beckett presses his lips together, the veins on his arms bulging.

I stare at him with my mouth open, wondering what the fuck kind of meetings he has. This was our meeting. We were supposed to approach Andrew and ask him about his thoughts of joining the Silverstein Pack, and it's like Beckett lost his nerve.

I wiggle from Jordan's arms and stride to Beckett, snatching him by the wrist and yanking him to me, dragging him to the corner of the office.

I stand on my tiptoes and get in his face, breathing in his citrusy scent. "What are you doing?" I whisper, my voice hissing with the words. "Have you changed your mind?"

Beckett sighs, his breath tickling my mouth. "No, but I realize that it has to be you. You need to talk to him. He sees you as our leader. Not me."

We both know why. Because technically Beckett isn't our leader, though he is my alpha. And now he wants me to flex my power.

I never thought it would be this way. It's easier to demand alphas to do what I want to better our territory. But this is entirely different. This is basically asking him to marry me.

I know it's common practice for alphas. At least, it happened before the pack wars, but I never expected it to be me in charge. The Silversteins were a happy accident and a perfect example of destiny. But Andrew?

Maybe it's the same. Damn. Why am I so nervous?

"What if he rejects me?" I ask, realizing that the idea of being rejected pains me. It's not something I've ever had to think about.

"He won't. He'd more likely reject me." Beckett swallows, the room absolutely silent as we whisper to each other. All eyes remain glued to us.

"I can't do this." I close my eyes and inhale a soft breath, trying to silence my unbidden negative thoughts. How embarrassing would it be for the leader of a territory to ask a man to be on her pack only to have him say no?

"You can. If you feel as if you can't, then we won't proceed. I don't want you being uncomfortable about this." Beckett rubs his fingers over my cheek, playing with my pale blond hair.

I narrow my eyes, his words daring me to prove him wrong. Because I'm not uncomfortable. I just... This is all so weird. But it's not exactly bad. Just new.

"I'm not uncomfortable. I just—" I heave a breath and straighten my shoulders, accepting his dare. He wants me to take charge, so I will. His words were enough to want me to resist my innate nature to obey and to sit back and allow others to do things for me. This is all just some growing pains as I take the reins and my throne to heart.

Leaning in, I kiss him softly, teasingly, hoping he thinks about this kiss the entire time he is away from me. I want my affection to linger on his mind. I want him to crave me while I'm with Andrew. It would serve him right. It'll truly show me if this is what is best for everyone.

I flick my gaze to my betas. "Make sure you guys aren't late. I need you all by my side."

Because I know what I have to do. I have to make it clear to the Pack Regimes that they don't control me. I'm an equal to them. I'm more than my order. I'm more than what everyone thought I was supposed to be.

"Andrew," I call, standing in front of my full-length mirror. "Can you help me?"

I should've just been honest the moment my pack left me with Andrew, but I lost my nerve and told him that I had to change into something more appropriate for a meeting with the Pack Regime. It wasn't true, but I needed to buy myself some time to get my mind in the right place.

Andrew peeks his head into my wardrobe, his eyes locking on mine in my mirror. I hold up my dress with one hand, the zipper opened down to my lower back, exposing my skin. He drinks me in without comment, slowly sauntering closer.

"You look beautiful," he says, his voice even as he stops behind me, his eyes shining in the lights.

I don't turn to look at him, remaining frozen in place. The heat of his body warms me even without him touching me. I imagine what it would be like. If he'd be gentle. If his fingers would be rough from the years of his experience working with different pack authorities. It's as if Beckett's confession has awakened something new inside me. Something I had focused on resisting.

"Thank you," I murmur, my body humming with his closeness, his sweet candy scent as alluring as his warmth. I take a step back, bumping into him, the air suddenly thick around us.

I swear sparks erupt from his fingers, his strong hand grasping my waist to steady me. Blush crawls up my throat, reddening my face. I wonder if he senses my sudden attraction, growing by the second.

I spent many hours watching my brothers encourage each other with Kinsey, and I never really expected such a thing to happen to me. I can hear Jordan in my head, telling me to use my sex appeal to seduce this man. I can imagine Beckett caressing my cheek, encouraging me to do what I feel is right by our pack. He said it himself. He's seen how Andrew looks at me and how I reacted to such attention, even if it was on a more platonic level, just appreciating him as an alpha. His scent. His personality and how skilled he is.

"Holly..." Andrew's voice trails off, his thoughts a mystery to me.

I spin around and face him, our eyes locking on one another. "Can I ask you a question?" My mouth opens and spits out the words before I have a chance to think things through. I talk when I'm nervous, and it's been a while since I have felt this way. The last time was when I moved in with the Silverstein Pack. The first time we knew this was forever. But those nerves have faded, now only continuous excitement remaining.

Andrew releases a breath and rolls his shoulders, stepping back to put more space between us.

"Anything. You have to trust me completely, so I'm always open to you. I will never lie or be dishonest." He swallows and shifts on his feet. Is he nervous too? There's something about it that helps ease the butterflies swarming my stomach.

"Why did you want to be my bodyguard? I know that you came highly recommended by my family, but why? What about your pack?" I'm sure that he's told Beckett and the others his reasoning. He may have even told Wilder, Enzo, Arsenio, and Desmond. But it's something I want to hear for myself. I have to know in his own words now that he's not trying to impress anyone.

"I no longer have a pack. My brothers died in the territory wars. Casualties of one of the bombs. I was offered a position on the royal guard, and I thought why the hell not? I had no desire to live alone, and it's incredibly hard to find a new pack. Being a royal guard would have helped give me some ties and security for my future." Andrew remains expressionless, though I can see grief haunting his beautiful eyes. I've seen eyes like that before in my sister-in-law. Kinsey used to carry a blip of sadness about her that only my brothers could scare away, filling her with happiness.

And I suddenly want to do the same.

"I'm so sorry. It should've never been that way. It's a bunch of useless power trips. People shouldn't have died because some packs couldn't accept the fact that Saint Vista is changing." I wet my lips, my voice soft. "So, you were on my brothers' staff?"

I haven't even been home since I moved into this palace. I knew that there were some power shifts, but I have been so concerned with my own territory that I didn't think much about Gilded Sands.

"For a few months until this opportunity came up. I went to school with Enzo if you didn't know. We lost touch when he had to transfer to private."

The funny thing is Enzo didn't have to transfer to private because he was enrolled his whole life. He had managed to enroll himself in the public school without our father's knowledge. He had to return when he got caught. It's not easy for a prince to just stop showing up somewhere. People notice.

I smirk, the memory flooding back to me because I was so jealous. I wanted to pretend I wasn't an omega to join him. He would've helped me but this was before suppressants. They used to be illegal. And in some places, they still are.

"It wasn't until the announcement of the new leaders had I realized the truth as to why Enzo could suddenly afford private school back in the day. He had told me his pack was part of the police. Mostly betas. And then I saw his smug face on TV. I had nothing to lose, so I reached out to him." Andrew breathes softly, his scent still so heavy around me. "He's the one who suggested I apply for this position. He thought I'd be happier. I was better fitted for something that wasn't patrol."

I wonder if Enzo had known about the Silversteins' concerns. Why wouldn't he? I know Beckett confides in my brothers, especially when it comes to his responsibilities. None of us were born to lead. In our minds, we were just to do as we were told. There was always someone above us to give direction, and now that we are in that position, it's hard to break old habits.

"Are you? I know it hasn't been long, but I know it's a lot. I sometimes question whether or not this is all worth it. If I can even manage." I drop my gaze to the front of Andrew's button-up, studying the fabric as if it's the most interesting thing in the world.

Mostly, I need to redirect my attention. It's as if his eyes manage to pull the truth from me unintentionally. I hadn't realized how comfortable I was in his presence until now. He feels safe. Trustworthy.

Warm fingers caress my cheek, his unexpected touch igniting a fire inside me. One that blazes through me, devouring every ounce of hesitation.

"Never let someone else's expectations of you define your capabilities. You're incredibly strong, Holly. With your history and everything that keeps coming your way...even the strongest alpha would struggle." Andrew's low voice lures my attention back to him. "I wouldn't have taken this position if I didn't believe you were capable of fulfilling your duties. I'm here to ensure that you can. I know about the concerns your pack faces. Many expect you to fail, and I'm anxious to see you prove them wrong. To show all of the assholes who feel entitled because of their order that it means nothing. I truly believe our society will be so much better off with you guiding it."

I press my hand to my chest, his words digging deeply into me in the best way possible. I never expected such a compliment.

Something breaks inside me, my knees weakening, my body wanting nothing more than to throw itself at Andrew. I ignore my reserve and slide my hands up around his shoulders, standing on my tiptoes to close the space. His eyes widen for a split second, and then his features blur as my mouth finds his. I kiss him, giving in to the wild attraction that has been brewing since the day he saved my life.

He doesn't move. He doesn't return my affection either, and my fluttering heart stills in my chest before hardening to drop into my stomach.

I pull away in embarrassment, a dozen thoughts racing through my mind. Andrew touches his lips as if he can still feel mine, and his eyes remain wide with fear.

"I—I'm sorry. I shouldn't have done that." I turn away and face the mirror, resting my palms on the cool glass.

"Holly..." Andrew's words fade, his thoughts remaining a mystery to me.

"It's okay. You don't have to say anything. It wasn't supposed to go like this. What you said... That was very kind of you." I reach behind me, trying to pull up the zipper of my dress, still halfway down.

Andrew steps closer behind me and helps me in silence. His presence doesn't help my wild emotions, and I squeeze my eyes shut, begging them to cooperate and not start filling with tears.

"Holly," Andrew repeats, his voice barely over a whisper. "Can you turn around?"

Can I? Maybe. Do I want to? I'd rather the ground open up and swallow me whole. What if this supposed attraction

Beckett saw was not what he was thinking? What if it was just friendliness?

Gently grasping my shoulders, Andrew turns me around to face him. His expression morphs from shock to something darker, sexier. If I continue to look at him, I might kiss him again. This is the same feeling I get every time I look at Beckett. It's hotter than my sweet love for my betas. More carnal. It's as if my very being knows that he can satiate me on a level not everyone can.

I exhale a slow breath, my eyes blurry. "You probably think I'm crazy. Or that I'm a horrible person. It isn't what it looks like. I love the Silversteins. I have bonded with Beckett."

"I know you have, and I don't think you're a horrible person. I think you're beautiful and compassionate. I overheard the five of you talking." Andrew rubs his lips together, his hand still resting on my shoulder while his other one slides through mine. "I'm absolutely honored that you feel as if I would make a good member of your pack. I just—"

"It's okay. You don't have to say anything." I can feel his rejection already coursing through me, causing my heart to thunder in a way that makes me feel as if I'm dying. This was so ridiculous of us. No sane man would want to join a pack that isn't even officially bonded under the law of the region.

I slip away from Andrew and turn toward the secret door

that'll lead to the tunnels. I can't stand the thought of someone seeing me cry over a dumb rejection. I don't know what's worse. The fact that I overestimated myself in my abilities or the fact that I have let my pack down. It's not even about me, really. Beckett needs this. He made it clear that he doesn't feel as if he'll make a good leader otherwise. He's afraid without the help of another alpha that he'll fail me. But it's not him who will fail. It's me.

"Holly, wait." Andrew tries to grab my hand, but I tug away and slap it against the wall opening the door.

I don't wait. I'm not in a good place to hear what I'm sure is a good excuse.

I don't need excuses.

I just need space.

I need to figure out what to do next.

I need to ensure things go how we want.

If only I had guidance. If only there was another omega I could talk to who has been in this position.

But I'm the one who must forge the way for the future.

I must be an example for others to follow. I need to prove that an omega can reign. That an omega can do anything.

I just have to believe it myself. I can do anything.

I will do anything.

15

Beautiful Omega

ANDREW

I fucked up. I fucked up so badly that I'm not sure I can ever come back from this. Holly rushes into the panic room leading to an underground area safe from the rest of the world. The door closes and locks behind her, and I race to slam my hand against the security pad.

It beeps and turns red instead of opening.

God damnit.

This was the only one I hadn't checked to make sure it would read my handprint. Holly hasn't been in her suite nearly this entire time, but she finally decided to return here, claiming there was a specific dress she wanted.

I didn't question it, because I had known about the man who died in here. She has so many other outfits scattered within the rooms of her packmates. I don't claim to understand women either. So here I am, standing in her wardrobe, surrounded by her scent, wishing I could kick myself a thousand times for letting her make it into the corridor without me.

I'm an asshole.

I was so caught off guard by her delectable kiss that my brain shut down and all I could think about was how much I wanted her to continue. But my body froze. My thoughts shouting that kissing her should be illegal.

Any other pack would murder me for even touching their omega, but the Silversteins are different. They're as different as the Gilded Sands Pack, and it has taken me a bit of time to get used to it.

I had no idea how serious they were, hearing the five of them talk about inviting me to join them. I didn't even comprehend what that would mean. I thought that because I'm Holly's bodyguard that it would continue to be more platonic. I thought perhaps it was just a power move.

But she kissed me. Me.

Her lips opened up a part of me that I had nailed shut. I

never in my wildest dreams believed that an omega would give me her attention. My dreams of a family and a pack died with my brothers. I had expected a life of loneliness.

My reaction to her affection pretty much guarantees it.

I stare at the metal door, wondering what the fuck I'm supposed to do next. She should never be out of hearing range. I don't even know which direction Holly ran.

Sucking up my shame, I pull out my cell phone and tap the screen. It rings and rings, Beckett not picking up right away. He's always the first one I'm supposed to call if there's a problem. I hang up and click on Wesley, Beckett's second in command.

I don't get a chance to connect the call because a text message pops up on the screen.

Beckett: I have added you to the wardrobe security. Holly is in the panic room down by the kitchen.

I turn my attention toward the ceiling, spotting the security camera.

Fuck my life.

I don't even want to think about the fact that Beckett probably saw everything.

He probably didn't answer his phone because if I were him, I'd be pissed off. I've probably offended the entire Silverstein Pack all because my dumb brain wanted to glitch on me.

Me: Thank you.

I consider typing out a dozen excuses, but he's not the one that needs to hear me out. Holly is our leader, and she is the one that matters most.

Beckett doesn't respond, and I tuck away my phone and slap my hand to the security pad. I enter the short corridor that leads directly into the small apartment-like panic room. I find the other door across the way, hidden in a tall cupboard and enter into the tunnels that wind through the palace. Security cameras blink every dozen feet, and I cringe at the fact that Beckett probably watches my walk of shame. I keep my head up, staring ahead of me as I make my way down to a set of stairs that'll take me to the panic room Beckett told me Holly was in.

I stop at the metal door, inlaid into the wall without a handle or anything and just stare at it. What am I supposed to say to her? I'm afraid of what I'm about to walk into. Facing brutal, murderous alphas is easy compared to this. I can handle myself when it comes to people who try to put you in your place. I have looked down the barrel of several guns, and even then, it doesn't compare to the anxiety I have now.

Hurting an omega's feelings is one of the worst offenses in my book. It's one of the reasons why I gladly took the position as Holly's bodyguard. I wanted to be able to protect her from evil men—the type of man I have apparently become.

I raise my hand to knock on the door, not even knowing if Holly would be able to hear it. I want to give her enough of a warning to hopefully help her steel herself against me. It would be utter torture if she doesn't, but I would deserve it.

Banging my fist, I wait a moment before pressing my hand to the palm pad. The door clicks and swings inward an inch, giving me the leverage I need to push it all the way open. I don't see Holly immediately, and I wonder if I have the wrong room.

But then a small whimper strikes me right in the heart, stealing my breath away.

The coward in me wants to run, but the protector in me closes the door and strides forward into the room.

Holly doesn't come out from her hiding spot, and I stop in the middle of the room and look around. The couch and bed are both empty and so is the table. I noticed that the pillows are missing from the furniture, and I spot a desk in the corner of the room with the chair pushed out.

Holly's bare feet peek out from the desk where she has created a nest to bury herself in. My heart aches at the sight of her. The sole reason she's doing this is for comfort because I caused her such distress. This is why I'm unfit to be a part of her pack. If I were good enough for her, we wouldn't be in this position in the first place. I wouldn't be standing here, listening to the soft whimpering cries of the most beautiful omega I've ever seen in my life. One that shouldn't be mine. I lost my chance when I lost my pack.

"Holly?" I ask, shuffling closer, trying my best not to let my nerves get the best of me. I have never felt this kind of fear. My weakness happens to be tears. It's as if my brain implodes at just the sight. Especially because I don't know how to make them go away. She is not mine to comfort. She is not mine to hold or to make promises to.

And it kind of pisses me off. I'm torn between what is right, and what I want.

"I didn't mean to upset you," I add, standing beside the desk.

Again, she doesn't respond, staying hidden with a blanket covering the entrance. I have never seen an omega's nest before. It's such a luxury to be this close with her in a place she feels safe. I wish I wasn't the one responsible for sending her running here.

Plopping on the floor, I pull my knees to my chest and rest my chin on them. "I was an idiot. I wish I could explain why I reacted like I did, but none of it really justifies the fact that I hurt you. That's the last thing I ever wanted to do. It is my job to protect you."

"I understand. You didn't sign up to be assaulted by an omega. It was wrong for me to assume anything." Holly sniffles, her shaking voice like a burning knife to the chest, slowly cutting out my heart to bleed all over me.

"You didn't assault me. If I didn't want your affection, I would have easily avoided it. And that's my problem. I'm so attracted to you. So much so that I wish I could turn back time and react more appropriately." It's as if her closeness drags my desires from me, my heart battling against my mind and what I know I should do. I should reject her. I'm not in a place to suddenly start making plans for my future involving her. I should let her down easy and take a more practical approach.

But I've never been good at doing what is right. I will always do what feels right to me.

And that's Holly.

"So I wasn't misreading you? I'm sure I could've handled this better, it's just...I don't know what I'm doing. I have always had my decisions made for me. And now that I can make them for myself, I'm just..." Holly pulls at the blanket, dropping it from the opening of the desk where she sits sideways among pillows.

I've never seen her look so vulnerable. She's always carried herself like a true leader, guarded and powerful, never hesitating when it comes to danger. A part of me hates myself for doing this to her. She shouldn't be hiding. She should be yelling at me for my idiotic behavior.

Crawling closer, I shove myself into the small space to get a better look at her. Her bittersweet scent, like coffee and vanilla, permeates the small space. Her delectable fragrance gets to me in a good way, and I inhale a small breath, holding it on my palate.

Something steals away my good senses, maybe her closeness, her scent. My desire. It gives me the push I need to stretch closer and touch her cheek, smearing the tears away. Her gaze travels from my eyes to my lips. Her fascination with my mouth sends desire traveling right to my cock, hardening my body. The fact that she doesn't scream at me to leave the space speaks volumes. She considers me safe. It's something I didn't know that I needed. I knew it was an expectation, but I also knew that such feelings have to be earned, and I thought I ruined it.

"I would like to kiss you," Holly says, her voice soft and alluring.

I swallow at her comment. She's giving me another chance, and I can't fuck it up despite my brain screaming that this shouldn't be happening. I'm not a part of her pack. I have no one. I don't deserve an omega.

Stupid fucking head. I'd rather listen to my heart.

I close the space to her, her mouth sweeter than her scent, and I kiss her softly, exploring her pouty mouth until she parts her lips and glides her tongue across mine, kissing me deeply.

It's a kiss that awakens a deep-seated need in me, one that I thought died with my pack. And I crave Holly so desperately that I want nothing more than to call her mine.

If we weren't in such a small space, I'd pull her closer, on top of me. I imagine what it would be like to feel her body wrapped around mine. The heat of her desire dripping over me. It steals my breath away, and I pull back and smile, rubbing my thumbs across her cheeks, hoping that she feels what her affection ignites inside me.

"I want to start over, Holly. I know that it will be difficult to forget my poor judgment, but I want you to know that I'm open to your wants. I just...it's hard to explain. My past haunts me. I can't promise that I'll always say the right thing to you. I'm not good at getting out of my own head. It's going to take time." I need to be upfront with her. I know it's what she wants.

"Time is one of the few things I know how to give. I'm patient. I'd like to properly introduce you to the Silversteins. I know that you're familiar with them, but this is different. It isn't about you being my bodyguard. It's about possibly joining our leadership. Our pack." Holly fidgets, playing with the tips of her pale blond hair. "If that's okay. I know it's weird. We kind of just threw this out there."

I lift and drop my shoulders. "It was quite the surprise but a good one. Let me help you finish getting ready, and we can discuss everything after the meeting with the Pack Regimes."

She nods her head and smiles, her face lighting up and so beautiful. I almost wonder if this is a dream. Something I might wake up from. The thought clenches my heart.

This is real.

This is happening.

Now I just have to ensure that I never let anyone down. It's time for me to prove myself.

I am a worthy alpha.

Now if only I can truly believe it.

Only time will tell.

Omega's Reign

HOLLY

I thought I was prepared for this meeting. I had a mental list of things I wanted to discuss with the Saint Vista Pack Regimes. The first one being how to handle the Righteous Waters Pack and if I should just put out a search to bring them before us for judgment. The second I stepped into the quiet meeting room, I realized that might be a mistake. We—my brothers and I—are in this position because we took it. We didn't give anyone else a choice, not like they'd have done the same. We are all a little off-kilter when it comes to morals.

Though some of us want equality and will fight for it. Others just want the power. It's obvious that trust is nonexistent in this room.

So for now, Righteous Waters is solely my problem. I will not be seeking advice from anyone outside of my family and my pack.

As for the other things? I guess I'll find out.

Glancing at Andrew, I bite my lip and motion for him to stay outside. There are no bodyguards for anyone who isn't on the Pack Regimes allowed in the meeting. I close the door and turn toward the male-dominated table apart from one woman alpha who has taken over the territories of Starlight Horizon and Ginger Rain. Only one of my brothers, Arsenio, sits among them, the rest of my brothers choosing to give him control this time. They all agree on everything together, but they also don't find it necessary to be present at every meeting.

I expect to find Beckett, but two empty seats greet me on the far right of the long table. He's not here. They won't wait for him either, because he is only my consultant. I'm the true leader of Platinum Shores.

I reach into my bag and pull out my cell phone. I don't care if everyone stares at me.

Me: Where are you?

I slow my walk to the table, staring at my screen, hoping that

Beckett replies quickly that he's on his way.

Arsenio stands up and pulls out my chair, giving me a quick hug. Why am I so nervous? I've been in front of these people several times over the last few months. They're not my superiors. We're on equal levels.

"It's nice to see you again, Holly," Armand says, keeping his hands together on the table. He's the leader of Midnight Meadows and one of the few original Pack Regime leaders.

I nod, offering him a smirk. "I would say the same, except I recently overheard a conversation between my brother and my alpha."

I should wait until everybody gives their updates, but I can't help myself. I'm still fuming about the fact that Beckett had intended to propose to me but the rest of the leaders have been playing games about it.

Armand leans forward, turning his gaze toward the other leaders. "Would you care to elaborate? I would prefer not to make any assumptions before giving an explanation."

I sigh in annoyance. "You and the others have not approved of a formal bonding for me and the Silversteins. Beckett has been wanting to propose to me for a while. What the fuck gives?"

Cameron's chair squeaks, drawing my attention to him. The Shadow Palms leader has always been pretty neutral toward other territories outside of his own. "We never said you couldn't bond and marry the Silversteins—"

"But you haven't approved of their status change. They're still considered my advisors." I stand up from my seat, pulling an alpha move to loom over everyone sitting. I don't know how effective it is, considering I'm an omega, but I try anyway. "I'm completely offended by this. You claim I'm an equal to you, yet you act as if my position of power is temporary."

"That's not—"

I smack my hands on the table. "Stop lying! You have only agreed to this because of my brothers. You—"

"Settle down, Holly. You're overacting." Spencer steeples his fingers, his smug face annoying me. He usually remains quiet and only talks when a vote is needed. He has no allies or enemies in the region, keeping his position because of it.

"We think you're sending mixed signals to the territories. You want to be treated as an equal yet you reject your order. You suppress your nature as if you don't want it." Armand scratches his fingers through his hair. "You're not leading by example."

I stand frozen in shock, his words resonating through me. What does he mean that I'm not leading by example? I have ensured that I acted like an alpha. I have put the leaders in their places, showing them just how powerful I am. I haven't rejected my order. I have proven that I am just as strong and capable as an alpha even though I'm an omega.

"Are you kidding me? I set an amazing example for my people. They know that I'm just as powerful as an alpha. They respect me." How truthful that is? It depends on who you ask. I just know that I can handle anything thrown at me.

"That's my point. You are acting like an alpha. You need to show the entire region that you are also capable of ruling as an omega. Starting by showing you're not afraid of yourself." Cameron sighs, dropping his gaze to the table.

I furrow my brows and look at Arsenio, wondering what the fuck this is about and if he knows.

I'm so confused.

"They are talking about the suppressant pills, little sis. They think that because you suppress your nature that you don't approve of your own order." Arsenio reaches out and takes my hand. "I happen to disagree. I think that you're capable of anything. It's not about your order but about you as a person."

"We just want our people to know that it's okay being an omega. It's been so long that so many hate their orders. So many refuse to even join packs right now. They don't believe things have changed, and we can tell them you're an omega, but nobody really believes us." Cynthia, the only other female on the Pack Regimes straightens her back. She's the first woman alpha in the leadership as well.

"So you will approve of my bonding with the Silversteins if I stop taking suppressants?" The weight of my question hangs heavy in the air, the rest of the leaders probably nervous about my response. "That shouldn't be a stipulation, you know."

"It's not a stipulation for you to be part of the leadership. But if you want a strong pack, you might want to consider all of your options." Armand crosses his arms over his chest.

I don't know how I feel about this.

What they are asking would mean me going into heat. It would mean children. It would mean showing the vulnerability that I have been suppressing. It would also show how different I truly am. A leader must be ready at all times for anything. I can't imagine myself in that position without repercussions.

But if it means the Silversteins will be approved as fit for ruling, then I'll do it. I will do anything for the men I love. I'm willing to even open myself up to another in Andrew.

I purse my lips. "I have a strong pack. They're capable of running Platinum Shores. I'm capable of leading regardless. I will prove it. I will stop taking suppressants, but it will only be temporary. I will show you that it doesn't change who I am. The only thing I'm suppressing is my ability to breed."

Arsenio stands up. "I don't agree with the stipulations. You know we need complete majority."

I raise my hand at my brother. "It's fine. I'm capable of making my own decisions and handling this. But before I leave, you must guarantee my bonding."

The other members of the Pack Regimes nod their heads, silently agreeing.

"Is there anything else? I will submit the census for my territory in a few days. I'm almost satisfied with the alpha leaders." I look at each of the alphas before me.

None of them returned my stare except for Arsenio.

He doesn't look happy, but he doesn't have to be. This is my decision. If this is what they want, then this is what they get.

They're going to see what it means for an omega to truly reign.

Beckett: I'm so sorry I missed the meeting. We had a lead on Hector. I had to take it.

Me: You should've told me.

Beckett: You have enough to worry about.

Holly: I'll talk to you later.

Beckett: Holly...

I tuck my phone into my bag and lean back in the passenger seat next to Andrew. He's been silent since I left the meeting room, stomping my way to the elevator. I'm shaking because of the interaction with the alphas. A part of me is so pissed off. How dare they try to manipulate me by using my order against me—claiming that I'm the one who has a problem. That's far from the truth. The only problem I have is that I have to prove myself at all. They wouldn't question me if I happened to be an alpha.

They probably wouldn't question the Silversteins if they were all alphas. But Beckett is the only one. I see why he wanted to bring another member to our pack. But now? I don't even know if it'll make a difference. I don't even know if Andrew would truly want this life. I'm not even sure I do. But my pride won't let me give up. Like the other leader said, I have to set a good example. I need to show other omegas that they're not beneath anyone. They're not intended just to breed. To satiate an alpha's needs. We are meant for more. Like my brothers have always said, an alpha is nothing without their omega.

"Where to, Holly?" Andrew asks, breaking the silence. I'm pretty sure he'd stay here with me all day if I didn't say anything. He wouldn't make any decisions without my prior approval. He respects me as much as the Silversteins.

I tilt my head back and rest it on the headrest. "Away from here. I don't care."

"Back to the palace?" he asks, seeking confirmation.

I lift and drop my shoulders. "No, not there."

He shifts in his seat and nudges me with his hand. "You have to be more specific. We can't just drive around. It's not safe."

Groaning, I bow forward and let my blond hair cascade over my face. "Take me to the omega compound." I haven't been in weeks, entrusting Beckett's sisters to handle the packless omegas as they wait for their chance to find alphas they adore and who will care for them in the way they need.

I know that I've been taking longer than expected to have my shit together, but I wanted to make sure that everything was perfect for them. And the fact that my current alpha leaders in Platinum Shores have lied about the state of their omegas pisses me off. It makes me worry about trusting anyone with these men and women who need protectors. They need someone safe and helpful. And right now, I only see myself as that someone.

"Sure thing." Andrew puts the car into drive and reverses from the parking spot. He turns on soft music to help fill the silence.

I shift and stare out the window, watching the buildings go by as we leave the one neutral territory that all of the Pack Regimes share. There are only betas in Golden Woods, and everyone leaves each other alone. This would be the place I would run to if I were hiding my order. It makes me wonder how many hidden omegas thrive here without anyone really knowing.

They will show themselves if and when they're ready. That's why the rest of the leadership doesn't concern themselves with it.

It takes over an hour to return to the borders of Platinum Shores, my territory formerly a part of another region. I'm closest to Gilded Sands but the farthest away from anyone else. Luckily most of my border is shoreline and easy to protect.

Not that there are any wars happening. Our region is still reeling from the last.

Andrew rests his hand on my knee, gently drawing my attention to him. In his peripheral vision, he offers me a smile while keeping his gaze on the road. I never thought I could be comfortable with another man outside of the Silversteins, but I also never thought I would be an omega ruler either.

It's the kind of good surprise that I love in life. It's what helps me keep my focus on the future.

My thoughts wander to what I'm getting myself into, weaning myself off the suppressant pills. I'm not ready for children, so I'll have to figure it all out. My heat will come, and if I fully succumb to my nature, I could have the kind of surprise I'm not ready for.

"Beckett's calling," Andrew says, tapping the screen on the dashboard. "Do you want me to—"

Slamming the brakes, Andrew fishtails, the vehicle shaking like crazy. I whip my attention to the road, spotting a black van burning rubber in front of us.

I don't get a chance to ask Andrew what's going on before something thuds against our trunk, jolting the sedan.

My body cools at the sight of Hector wielding a gun. He aims it at the back window.

Glass sprays everywhere.

Dangerous Past

HOLLY

"Stay down," Andrew commands, stomping the gas pedal, sending us barreling forward toward the black van.

Something plinks off our car, the bang of metal startling me.

It takes everything in me not to try to sneak a peek. But I know what monster lurks behind us. What calamity lies before us.

Jerking the wheel, Andrew turns left, cutting across the empty street to zoom down an alley. A car blocks the alleyway exit, stopping us in our tracks. We've been trapped. Hector's psychotic laughter echoes through the air, coming in through the broken back window.

"Holly, get the gun out of the glove compartment. There is an alcove to the right. Do you see it?" Andrew motions with his head, keeping his gaze split between the car blocking us in and Hector coming up from behind.

I pull the gun from the glove compartment and unbuckle my seatbelt, trying my best not to give away anything if Hector's focused on me. "I see it."

"I want you to get out as soon as I pass. I will distract Hector. When you get the chance, I want you to run. Trust no one. I will find you." Andrew lightly steps on the throttle, navigating slowly toward the other vehicle.

I don't argue with Andrew and instead do as he says, counting the seconds until I pass the alcove. I shove open the door and slam it, ducking into the small hiding place. The second I do, Andrew shoves the car into reverse and stomps the throttle, sending it hurdling backward. Hector fires his gun, trying his best to stop Andrew. Jumping out of the way, Hector smashes himself to the wall, narrowly missing getting pulverized by the vehicle.

I take my chance and aim my gun, firing at the vehicle blocking the alleyway exit. The driver is far too focused on Andrew that he doesn't see me, and I shoot him through the open window. I never thought I would be the one with so much blood on my hands. My brothers were always the ones dealing with this shit. But this is what I have to do. I knew better than to believe that I could take a position of power without any issues.

And I need to take care of this one quickly and quietly. The last thing I need is for the Pack Regime leaders to find out.

The man behind the wheel groans and tries to pull out of his seatbelt. I should end his life immediately, but I can't keep dealing with unexpected surprises. The longer Hector is at large, the longer it will take for me to relax.

I run around the hood and to the driver's side, yanking the door open. I aim my gun at the man's head, pressing the barrel hard to his temple.

"Give me the location of the Righteous Waters Pack," I demand, grinding my teeth with my anger.

The man doesn't respond, clutching the side of his neck. Blood pours through his fingers, the gunshot wound most likely fatal. He won't be able to tell me either. This is pointless.

"I'll show you their location." A hand grabs my shoulder before I have a chance to spin around. Fingers lock through my hair, yanking tightly against my scalp.

I catch the reflection of the alpha in the shiny paint of the car. "Let me go," I growl, forcing my weight to the ground. I refuse to make it easy for him.

"Don't fight. You don't want me to hurt you, do you?" he asks, keeping his voice low.

My mind whirls. I'm not one to bow. I will not submit.

I'd rather go down swinging.

But if I do, I'm taking this alpha with me.

Never Bow

HOLLY

Always target the soft spots.

Wilder's words swirl through my mind as I strategize the best way to break free of this man's hold. I need to shift my body weight in a way that he can't control. If his focus is on keeping me restrained, it'll open him up for my attack. And I'll attack hard.

Shoving me forward, he smashes my chest against the back-door of the vehicle. I take the chance and charge backward, using the car as leverage. He's trying to pull the driver out so he can get in with me. If he manages, I might not escape. I'll face more injury. He obviously doesn't want to kill me. He'd rather torment me for the rest of my life.

"You fucking bitch," he growls, tightening his fingers through my hair even more.

Instead of grabbing at him, I clench my teeth and drop to my knees, feeling the pain of some of my hair ripping free from my scalp. He doesn't expect my move, and it knocks him off balance enough that I can push his leg. The man stumbles, dragging me with him, and I close the space and wrap my arms around one of his legs and lock my legs around his other one, pinning him in place. He can't move without falling. I look up at him as he bares his teeth, his face distorting with his anger. He releases my hair and tries to snatch at me, but I rock my body. He can't keep his balance any longer and falls back on the concrete. I scramble away instead of trying to fight him, and I crawl toward my gun now lying next to the car.

The man rushes me, but I'm faster. I swivel and shoot without hesitation. The bullet flies past him, hitting the window of a building. It's hard to get a good aim from my position. I shoot again, this time sinking the bullet in his thigh, missing my target by a few inches. I should aim for his stomach or chest, but the sadistic part of me wants to ensure that he suffers.

Hollering, he dodges out of my way and around the car,

climbing into the passenger seat. He's a coward just as I suspected. He will only fight when he knows he has the power. But I'm in control now.

The driver's side door flings open, and the body of the other man falls to the ground next to me. It's enough to get me moving. I rush to my feet, wanting nothing more than to stop this man from running. I want him to know what it's like to be chased. To feel as if he's powerless. Because he is. I have taken power, and I will never give it back.

I grab the wheel with one hand and press the barrel of my gun to his head with the other. "Tell me where you're staying. I'll make your death quick if you do."

The guy stills, his chest rising and falling with his heavy breathing.

"Fuck you," he growls. "Hector will get you. You can pretend to be an alpha bitch all you want, but it doesn't change who you really are."

I tense and pull the trigger, wanting to just end him. It clicks but nothing happens. The gun's out of bullets and I don't have another clip. The man realizes my mistake, and he tries to grab my hand. I swing and jam my thumb into his eye, feeling the soft wetness of his socket swallow my thumb.

He hollers and jerks away, blindly grabbing for the gear shift. He's going to drive away, and there's no way I can follow him on foot. Doing the only thing I can think of, I smack him in the face again, giving myself the moment I need to toss my cell phone into the car. He won't give me his pack's location, but I will find it. I will put them in their places. This is enough to lock them up without question. This is enough to enact a death sentence and wipe them off my territory.

I scuffle back, managing to keep my balance as I hit the curb and spin toward the wall of the building. The man doesn't bother trying to get me and stomps the throttle, sending the car forward.

I don't wait to see if anyone else comes for me and dash toward the main street. I just need to find a beta that I can borrow a phone from. It shouldn't be that hard. This is my territory after all. My people know who I am. If they want to be rewarded, they will help me. This is the type of area where it's easy to buy loyalty if I can't earn it.

Pounding my feet to the ground, I run faster and faster, putting as much space between me and the alley where I left Andrew with Hector. He said he would find me, but I don't know how since I tossed my phone. The best way is to just get to safety first.

A car horn blares, startling me, and I don't see the pile of trash. I trip and skid across the pavement, my arm burning with road rash.

"Oh, my God!" a feminine voice yells from somewhere to my right. "Holly!"

I try to crabwalk backward and hit my head against something hard. My eyes shadow with my vision. "Leave me alone!"

"Holly, it's okay. It's me." Lilac's familiar voice wraps over me as Beckett and Jordan's sister comes into my view. "Isaiah! It's Holly."

The pain in my body worsens, and I close my eyes. Isaiah's scent engulfs me, stealing away my fight.

The world turns dark.

"Holly! Wake up. I know you want to sleep, but I need you to stay awake." Isaiah's voice is like a wave of relief crashing over me. How is he here?

Tears burn my eyes as my emotions get the best of me. My head pounds with each of my slow breaths, and I tilt my face slightly toward the sound of his voice.

"Hector," I manage to say, squeezing the tears from my eyes, the heat of them caressing my cheeks. "He's here. He's attacked us. He's somehow tracking me."

"Tell me what happened. I need to know everything. How far did you run? Just keep talking to me." Isaiah shifts me in his arms, keeping his attention solely on me. The world moves around us as someone drives a vehicle, and I suspect it might be Lilac. The hint of her scent trickles through the air, blending with Isaiah's.

"How are you here?" I ask instead of answering his questions, my heart still thrashing from my fear.

"We had a lead about Hector being in our territory. I thought Beckett told you before the meeting. Andrew—"

"Andrew!" I cry, the mention of his name flooding my memory back to me. "Fuck. He could be in trouble. We had to separate. We need to go back."

"You're hurt," Isaiah says, remaining expressionless. "You need medical attention."

"Turn around. That's an order!" I yell, sitting up straighter, ignoring the pain radiating through me.

Lilac slows the vehicle and turns around, heading back in the direction they found me. I try to focus on the road, wishing I had paid more attention to what was behind me than the world in front of me as I tried to get far away.

"We were in an alley," I say, leaning forward in the seat, trying to get a good view out of the windshield despite the hazy sun in my eyes.

"Do you remember anything else? The color of the buildings? Was it a dead end?" Isaiah lifts my hair, searching through the strands until he touches an aching spot on the back of my head.

I wince and recoil. "No. There was a vehicle on one side and Hector came in through the other. Andrew made me get out and he went after Hector."

"But you were hurt," Isaiah says, checking me over inch by inch. "You have some bruises that aren't from falling."

I slowly bob my head, but I don't look at him. He's already worried enough as it is. "I'm fine. You should see how hurt the other two guys are." I force myself to laugh at how cliché my comment sounds.

Isaiah remains stern-faced. "They are dead men."

"I guarantee one is for sure," I reply, swallowing the ick of killing a man once again.

Groaning under his breath, Isaiah slides his arm behind me and pulls me to him, hugging me tighter. He brushes his lips against my cheek, inhaling a soft breath. He's torn between pride and relief and anger. If he were an alpha, his scent would grow stronger in the air.

"I'm okay, though. My brothers taught me well. I'm not incapable of protecting myself." I tilt my head and caress my lips to his. "They wouldn't have thrown me into this position had they thought I wasn't a good fit."

"But you shouldn't have to always be fighting for every-thing. No one should be able to get even a finger on you, Holly.

I don't know what we're doing wrong. I knew we should have gone with you. Beckett is stressed. He can't get out of his own head. He wants to do everything himself so you don't have to." Isaiah rests his hand on my knee. "It's just so hard."

My heart aches at his admission. I had suspected that there was more to it than Beckett just having a lead. I wonder if he was afraid to face the Pack Regimes because he feels he has too many shortcomings to lead by my side. It doesn't help that the Pack Regimes have been denying him for months now. It ignites anger in me just thinking about it. All of this could have been avoided had they just told me exactly what was on their minds.

"If this is too much—"

"It's not. I'm sorry. I shouldn't have said anything. It's just I was so scared when I saw you." Isaiah pats the driver's seat, getting Lilac's attention. "Turn up here. There's been an alert of an accident."

I hadn't realized that Isaiah was partially focusing on his phone which now glows with a message.

He doesn't let me see it though and turns it slightly.

"An accident?" My heart will never recover, constantly bouncing around with my nerves. If there was an accident...

"There's our vehicle," Isaiah says, pointing toward the windshield.

Several bullet holes pepper the car, and the back window is completely smashed away like Hector shot it and glass flew everywhere.

Lilac pulls to a stop, and Isaiah flings the door open, climbing out without me. He shuts the door, attempting to keep me in my spot, but I go out the other side, spotting three people near the driver's side door. I spot the blood on the passenger's window, and I cover my mouth. Something terrible happened.

"Holly, go wait in the car," Isaiah commands, blocking me.

I shove against him, standing on my tiptoes. "Is he dead?" My voice cracks with my question. I can't see much from my spot. Just the blood. The aftermath of a fight.

"Please, princess. You need to let me handle this now." Isaiah touches my shoulder, and I cringe at the pain of his fingers caressing unseen bruises.

I shift out of his way, trying to push past him again.

Legs dangle out of the driver's side door. It's a body.

My heart freezes at the sight. I can't see anything else because people block the way.

"Andrew?" I ask, my voice ringing out. "Move. I need to see."

One of the betas frowns and shakes his head, stepping just a foot out of the way.

I drop to my knees with a gasp, the unfamiliar shoes not

belonging to Andrew. It's another guy. Another member of the Righteous Waters Pack.

But where is Andrew?

I spin and crash into Isaiah's open arms. "It's not him. We need to find him!"

The beta who let me see the aftermath crosses his arms. "I'll get the surveillance for you, Your Majesty—"

I ignore him and turn to Isaiah. "Call a meeting immediately. Put the entire territory on lockdown. Hector must be found. Now!"

Alpha Hunt

HOLLY

I sit in the throne room, my legs curled up to my chest as I stare at the empty pews before me. In this moment, I'm torn, wanting to reject my duties as a pack leader and just give away my position of power to someone who wants it. I thought this was the life of my dreams. I thought that I could make a difference. What I didn't expect was to meet an adversary every step of the way. Maybe this is why omegas don't lead. I'm just so tired. My heart hurts. I just want to go into my nest, curl up, and never see another stranger again.

But people count on me. I have to prove to not only the Pack Regimes that omegas are capable of doing anything, but I also must prove to myself that I'm the right omega to show the world.

Right now, I'm doubting myself and my abilities. I can fire a weapon. I can strategize a war. But I can't protect my own pack. I can't provide the protection that they require, because they have a deep-seated need to do the same with me.

We have our orders for a reason. If only omegas hadn't been taken advantage of for so long.

A knock sounds on the ornate doors before they crack open and Beckett stands in the entryway. I haven't seen him since his text message informing me that he wasn't coming to the meeting, and I'm caught between being angry and relieved that he's here. His stoic expression gives nothing away, and he strolls down the aisle, not giving me a chance to get up.

"Holly, I'm so sorry I failed you," Beckett says, his eyes glassing over with his words. "I should've been there. I just—I need to prove myself to the Pack Regimes. I wanted to handle this for you."

My soul aches at the sight of my alpha, sullen and begging me for forgiveness. He drops to his knees and hugs my legs, burying his face against my body. "Will you forgive me?"

I slide off my throne to kneel beside him and engulf him in

a hug, wanting nothing more than to feel his arms around me. My affection breaks him, and he sobs a soft cry, hiding his face against me. I've never seen Beckett so gutted that it brings tears to my eyes.

"Of course, I forgive you. I've never blamed you in the first place. None of this is your fault." I stroke my hand on his back, trying to smooth his shaking body. "I just wish that you would talk to me more Beckett. I thought we had an understanding. We're in this together. As a pack. You don't have to act alone."

He sighs, his body relaxing against mine. "I keep telling my-self that. I was just ashamed. I knew that you would confront the Pack Regimes about me, and—I don't know. I shouldn't feel so weak. I should feel strong and loved, cared for and cher-ished because you love me enough to face down other alphas. And now look what happened? You were hurt. Andrew is missing. Things are—"

"We got a signal!" Jordan's voice booms through the air, his appearance in the doorway obliterating my sorrow and refilling my body with hope.

Beckett doesn't hesitate to lift me up with him, gathering me in his arms.

"The GPS signaled at the north side. Two blocks from the Omega Sanctuary." Jordan waves his phone, showing the screen even though we can't see it from our spot. "I have our team heading out for surveillance now. We want to get a visual before we follow."

I frown, my brows puckering. "And what about Andrew's location? I thought you guys were going to search for his."

Jordan twists his lips to the side, clutching his phone tighter. He holds my stare, not giving much away, but I can tell that his answer will be the same as it was the last time I asked. "We still haven't gotten a location for him. His phone is offline."

I squeeze my eyes shut, digging my nails into the palms of my hands. "I'm afraid. He should've contacted us by now. What if something happened?"

"Don't think like that. Andrew is a smart man. I suspect he's tracking your phone too. It's what I would do." Beckett rubs his hand over the length of my back, adjusting me in his arms.

Beckett's right. It's the best I can hope for. Because an alpha like Andrew, one who is like Beckett, would do anything for an omega, and I know Andrew wants me to be his.

These hotheaded, overly protective men, have a deep desire to prove themselves to the world.

Now I'm going to have to prove that it's not necessary. It's not about being an alpha or omega. It's about being a pack.

It's about doing things together.

I'm ready to show them this.

I'm ready to help my pack rise. But to do so, others must fall.

"We have a visual. But it's not Hector. It's a beta watching the entrance of the Omega Sanctuary. He looks as if he's mapping out the place." Wesley watches his phone, the video feed displaying a man photographing the walls around the sanctuary.

"We should take him out immediately," Jordan says, pulling his gun from its holster. He's beyond strategizing and just wants to take things by force. I can't blame him. We have tried and tried again to do things in a more civil manner. It worked for a while until we had to flex our power to those who we want to help run our territory, but I highly doubt it will help against those trying to tear us down.

"No," Beckett says, holding his hand up. "He's the only one here, so we need to follow him." Because my phone must still be in the beat-up vehicle, now parked in the lot of a park next to the walled-in property.

"Agreed. The Righteous Waters Pack wants to kidnap the omegas we protect here. I think that's their ultimate goal if they feel like they can't take our territory." Isaiah frowns, his face reflecting exactly what I feel inside. The thought of these bastards hurting any omegas under my reign leaves me wanting to destroy the world.

It pushes me to think of the world outside of myself and

my pack. "I won't let that happen. They have already ruined enough things. They've already hurt too many omegas in their lifetime. I won't stand for it." Even if I have to take out each pack member myself. I realize I have it in me despite not wanting to. But anger and unfairness does that to someone. Inequality gives me more strength. I'm aware that I'm better off than many, and I need to use this to help those who can't help themselves.

"He's moving," Wesley says, drawing my attention back to the guy. He looks around the area and shoves his phone into his pocket. Bowing his head, the guy strolls away as if he's not a creep. He's obviously trying not to draw attention to himself and pulls his head up to obscure his ugly face. A man on the Righteous Waters Pack could never be attractive. Ever.

"Follow him. Don't let him out of our sight." Beckett motions to Isaiah to get out of the car. "Stay close. Don't lose him. We'll stay further behind."

A part of me doesn't want Isaiah leaving us, but another part of me knows that it's the best way to follow this guy, especially because he turns into a park that we can't drive through, the walking paths winding for at least a mile across grass between an archway of trees.

"Head around the block. There's a parking lot on the other side." Beckett points at the windshield, instructing Jordan, who sits behind the wheel.

Wesley keeps his attention focused on the world outside, sweeping the area by looking through each window over and over again. We all know how dangerous it is for us to be out here without an army of bodyguards at this point. But you can't sneak around with that many people. It's important that we keep things between us, considering how few we can trust. I sometimes think that all it would take is for me to turn my back on someone to find a knife between my shoulders. And I'm sure my guys feel the same. That's why our private quarters are off-limits. We only have a few people that watch out for us.

"Give me an update," Beckett says, hitting the button on his comm device. "I can't see you guys from here."

"He's staying on path. Not looking around. He just wants to get out of here," Isaiah says, his voice coming through the speakers for everyone to hear.

I bounce my feet, my nerves growing more intense the closer we get to the parking lot. It's where we found the vehicle and watched the guy head to the Omega Sanctuary from here.

"Do you think he's being watched?" I rub my lips together, wetting them. I wish I had a glass of water to busy my mouth, the dryness of my throat croaking my words.

"It doesn't matter if he is. We're going to fight the rest of those fuckers," Wesley says, speaking up without looking at me. He rests his hands on the dashboard, sitting in the passenger seat beside Jordan.

And he's right. Even if the guy has backup, it's not going to stop us. We have the advantage. This is our territory, and I have studied every inch of it on the maps. My guys explored it by foot and by car. We have access to all of the security feeds. We have allies among the people. If it came down to it, the betas would more likely help us than help the criminals. They've spent far too much of their life under the reign of monsters. Even though I might be one too, I'm the monster who destroys for a good reason, so we can rebuild.

"Looks like he's heading right back to the car. I doubt he has backup at this point. The Righteous Waters Pack isn't that big, and they wouldn't risk losing more members than necessary, knowing who owns this territory. As much as I wish they were, they're not stupid," Beckett says, holding the button for his comm device to allow Isaiah to also hear his thoughts.

Slowing down, Jordan pulls up to the sidewalk instead of entering the parking lot. There aren't many cars here today, considering it's a weekday and many packs work. If they have children, they wouldn't be out until the weekend when everyone could be together to protect them. This isn't the territory where people are comfortable being alone. It's why this one beta sticks out.

"You can return to us, Isaiah. I have a visual. We need to be ready for when he takes off. We're going to follow him back to his home base." Beckett opens the back door and steps out, shielding his eyes as he stares at the parking lot.

I catch sight of the hooded guy strolling toward where his beat-up car rests in the shade of a tree. The man pulls down his hood and glances around, but he doesn't really focus. Mostly just looking for bystanders, I guess. It's obvious that he's not a professional and was commanded to do this by Hector. He's probably disposable as well, considering he doesn't look like he brings much to the pack. At least, that's what an alpha like Hector would think about a beta.

The man finally slides behind the wheel, and something in the backseat catches my attention. I jump at the sight of a figure popping up from behind.

"Shit. Isaiah, someone's in the backseat. Go! We can't let someone kill him!" Beckett shouts, rushing from the vehicle without hesitation.

It's enough to distract the man, and he swings his attention in our direction. And that's when I realize I recognize the figure in the backseat. It's Andrew. He's alive. He was probably tracking this guy since we were separated, because my phone is still in the car.

My heart leaps with excitement.

I rush from the backseat and grab Andrew's attention, his eyes darting to me. The beta takes advantage of the distraction and swings out, the glint of a knife glittering in the beam of sunlight peeking through the shade.

I gasp and cover my mouth, watching as the tip slides across Andrew's cheek.

"No!" I scream.

The man swings his arm again.

Andrew disappears from view.

Pack Fights

HOLLY

Boots clomp on the pavement behind me as Jordan matches my pace. Wesley runs ahead with Beckett. The back door flings open, and Andrew rolls out, landing on his back. Isaiah reaches the vehicle first and grabs the man, hauling him out of the driver's side before he can take off. I push myself to move faster and drop to the ground beside Andrew.

Blood pours down his face from the cut, and I run my hands over him, searching his body for another stab wound. There's only a tear in the front of his shirt, and I exhale in relief and press my palms to the spot, feeling the quick thumps of his heart beating.

"You're safe," Andrew says, surprising me by swinging his arms around me, pulling me on top of him. "I thought I had failed you when I tracked you to this guy."

"I tossed my phone in the car because I didn't want to lose him. We need to find where the Righteous Waters Pack is hiding." I bury my face in the crook of his neck, listening to a scuffle behind us as Isaiah and Beckett subdue the beta. He's lucky he's not the guy I had an encounter with before, because I would murder him immediately. But I had injured him. I had shot him in the thigh, there's no way he could be out walking around right now.

"Do you know how proud and infuriated I am at you? I was so fucking scared, but I'm so glad you thought to do that. I didn't go back to the palace, because there was no way I was going to return without you." Andrew kisses my temple, the sensation igniting something hot inside me.

It's now that I realize how quiet the world is.

I peek up and catch sight of Beckett, Wesley, Isaiah, and Jordan staring at me with the beta restrained on the ground, something gagging his mouth to keep him from talking.

I wish we weren't out here. I wish the asshole wasn't on the ground a few feet away from me. A moment like this should be kept private. It should be something for my pack to process and enjoy without worrying about the rest of the world outside of us.

"Get used to it, Andrew. She's going to drive you wild," Beckett says, striding forward without missing a beat. We have already had this discussion about Andrew and how he felt we needed him. And now after feeling as if I was going to lose him, I know exactly how much I need him too. I want the time to get to know him properly. I want my pack to bond in a way I had never imagined. Because it was always supposed to be just us, and I had no idea that we were truly missing just one thing. Andrew.

"I look forward to it." Andrew holds his hand out, and Beckett helps him up, while Andrew continues to hold me in his arms.

The others circle around us, caging me in a muscular circle that I can't get enough of. It feels so perfect being with them, all of us together. It gives me the strength to keep pushing forward.

This is what I'm fighting for. I'm fighting for a pack. I'm fighting for others like me to have their own packs, who love and cherish them and give them everything they need. Everything they could ever want. A good life. A happy life.

I laugh and kiss each of them, wiggling in Andrew's arm

until he sets me on my feet. "We need to get ourselves together. It's not over."

"We can't exactly follow him, Holls," Isaiah says, glowering at the man from over his shoulder. "What do you think we should do now?"

"Give him an ultimatum. If he wants to live, he'll tell us where to find Hector." Jordan touches his weapon, the holster hidden under his arm beneath his jacket.

"I'm kind of in the mood to cut it out of him," Wesley says, pulling a knife out and aiming it at the guy.

"It would be payback too." Isaiah motions to the cut on Andrew's cheek.

I dab it with my shirt, glad to see it wasn't deep as it already starts to coagulate. "I'd be happy to assist. Guys like this need to be put in their places." I say it the way I do so he knows what it feels like to be considered beneath me. Only an alpha would talk to him like that. It should be extra annoying when it comes from an omega. "Pull down his pants. I know exactly where I plan to start."

The others remain expressionless, but Jordan breaks, frowning at me, probably imagining the pain I pretend to want to inflict. It's such a guy thing to feel bad over an appendage that some don't deserve to even have in the first place.

Damn. I am a monster. But this isn't about the act. It's

about the mind games that come along with it.

"My queen, don't you think that's a little—"

I bring my finger to Jordan's lips, cutting him off. "There is no mercy for those against us. Now yank down his fucking pants," I say, channeling my brothers' attitudes. This is something they would pull. Freaking out someone to get them to comply.

The beta on the ground thrashes, trying to spit out the gag from his mouth. The fabric, which I think might be a dirty shirt found in the car, doesn't fall free from his mouth.

I grab a blade from Wesley and slap it against my palm, strolling closer. With a sadistic grin, Wesley follows my lead, leaving the others standing in silence, ready to intervene only if they feel the need to.

Wesley grabs the man's waist, hooking his fingers to the buckle of his belt.

The beta thrashes harder, screaming, doing his best to fight even though his hands are bound.

I stand over him and smile. "Is there something you'd like to say?"

Wesley reaches out and grabs the fabric from the guy's mouth, yanking it free. The beta chokes and coughs, his eyes red and shining with tears, his fear palpable enough for me to smell, the odor disgusting.

"Please don't hurt me. I'll tell you where Righteous Waters is hiding. Just don't hurt me." The guy heaves a breath and grinds his teeth.

I stare at him for a minute, letting the seconds drag on, wanting him to feel the fear that every omega feels when they face the world each day if they don't have a loving pack.

"Please," he begs, his eyes dripping with tears.

I look at the others. "If this is a trick, you will pay."

"It's not. Please. I'll show you. I'll give you anything you want," the beta says.

I bend over and pat his cheek. "I know you will. I'm your queen."

Enemies

WESLEY

We have a visual. I can't believe we actually have a visual. These fuckers have been like ghosts, haunting us without us getting a good lock on them. It has made me question my ability in protecting our palace and our territory. It has also affected my trust. And when you can't trust anybody, it makes things a lot more difficult. There's more work involved. The last thing we need is to be going into a trap.

But Righteous Waters no longer has the resources that it used to. They can't just call up all their allies and get them to join in a fight against a reigning pack. That's what happens when you make deals with men who can't guarantee to follow through. Because Holly's father was not liked. He had a lot of enemies, and trying to use Holly to bribe an ally wasn't going to work.

Not when she has brothers that care about her.

Many people would probably think that Holly deserves this, because the Righteous Waters Pack was incarcerated for a crime they didn't commit, but just because it wasn't that particular crime, doesn't mean that they didn't deserve being behind bars. They still do. They're not innocent. And the fact that they are back for revenge proves it.

"They have a lot of nerve thinking that they can have a base in my territory." Holly places her hands on her hips, her arms akimbo as she stares at the video feed, showing Hector and two other guys leaving an apartment at the very edge of our territory.

"Who owns that building?" Isaiah asks, using his fingers to magnify the screen, glowering as if his looks could kill him. If only.

"It belongs to the Waze Pack. I've already contacted them, and they had no idea. All of the tenants and management are packless betas. They have agreed to assist us by giving us access to their security cameras and codes. We have keys to all the apartments too." Beckett scratches his neck and exhales a deep breath. He's been more agitated today, and I wonder if it has to do with the fact that Holly stopped taking her suppressant pills. It'll take a bit to get out of her system, but I know that her pheromones have already grown stronger. Her delectable coffee and vanilla scent is so damn palpable that I just want to taste her. If only we had time.

"Do we have everyone we need? We're not doing this alone. I don't care if you think we can handle it, I'm not putting all of us at risk." Holly sounds so sexy bossing us around. I can't stop myself from placing my hand around her side and pulling her into me.

"We have a small army ready. Ten people along with us. We've only counted seven members left, so it shouldn't be a problem. They won't even know we're coming." Andrew sets down his phone, showing the list of people. "I've arranged them myself. These are people I have worked with before and have relied on. They are good."

I nod my head, trusting that Andrew knows what he's doing. He has already worked on the Gilded Sands guard. I'm sure those people are coming from Holly's brothers' territory. Because they are more reliable. They know Holly. She was once their beloved princess before becoming my queen.

"I'm sure they are," Holly says, offering a smile. "We need to make sure that we're quick and discreet. I don't want the Pack Regimes to know. We have another meeting with them coming up, and I believe this is the one where they finally followed through with their approval for us as a pack. They have to. I'm not accepting any other answer." Holly pulls her hair up into a high ponytail and sticks what looks like a thin blade within the strands, the jeweled handle decorative.

"Damn straight, we're not. This territory is ours. We have earned it. We have proven ourselves," Beckett says, draping a leather jacket over Holly's shoulders, the thick material enough to protect her. It goes along with her bulletproof vest. We're not taking any chances as the six of us prepare to greet our team.

I kneel and help Holly lace her boots before spinning her around and lifting her onto my shoulders. Her melodic laughter chimes through the air, helping to settle my nerves. I would carry her around all day, every day, if she'd allow it. I'd be her personal throne to rule from.

Linking her fingers through my hair, she giggles and nudges me playfully with her boots. "Take me to the team."

Beckett shakes his head, his face not fully lighting up. "Easy now. We're only meeting with Dale."

Holly squeezes my neck between her thighs, the gesture getting to me in a good way. "Why only him? Don't you think it's important that we meet the entire team? It's how we build relationships."

"It's better for your safety if we wait until after. We don't want that sort of information getting out. I trust these guys with my life, but I wouldn't expect them to give up their lives if they're captured. If they don't know, then the information cannot be taken from them." Andrew pats Holly's knee, and she squeezes me again.

"I hate this," she groans, leaning forward just enough to press against the back of my head. My dumb ass imagines flipping her around and turning her annoyance into pleasure. If she weren't wearing pants, I'd probably try. I'm great at multitasking. I bet I could make her cream before we even hit the garage.

I don't get the chance to think more about it because Beckett motions toward the door, getting the rest of us in place. I set Holly down in front of me, keeping my hands on her waist. I plan on not letting her get even a foot away from me. The rest of our pack will surround her in a protective wall. I don't care if she thinks it's ridiculous. I know she can fight and handle herself, but she shouldn't have to.

"It looks like Hector has called everyone home. We've had a visual on every surviving pack member entering the apartment. This should be easy," Isaiah says, staring at his phone.

"Don't jinx us," Jordan says, smacking Isaiah on the shoulder.

I remain silent, guiding Holly forward, hoping she doesn't get lost in her thoughts. I can tell that the happiness I aroused in her slowly fades with each passing step until we meet Dale standing just outside the door that leads into the huge six-car garage.

An unfamiliar Jeep looms inside, the garage door open and ready for our exit. Jordan snatches the keys from Dale and jogs to the Jeep, claiming his seat behind the steering wheel. I'm glad for it. We could all argue over who the better driver is, but I'm content with taking a seat with Holly in the back. Four of us will be in the vehicle while the others ride crotch rockets, ensuring we're surrounded at all times. Isaiah kisses Holly before abandoning us for his bike. He starts it, the rumble of the engine echoing through the garage.

Andrew and Dale follow his lead, and me, Holly, and Beckett join Jordan. My nerves start getting the best of me. I suddenly feel like there's more we should do to prepare.

"I wish we didn't have to separate," Holly says, sitting in the middle, snuggled up against me.

I drape my arm over her shoulders and hug her. I don't have to agree with her because she already knows that's how I feel. How we all feel. But we don't really have a choice. This is the safest bet.

Jordan navigates the Jeep from the garage, and the others stay close on their motorcycles. Dale leads the way with Andrew at our side and Isaiah behind us.

I stay on guard, holding my gun with my free hand, occasionally meeting Jordan's gaze in the rearview mirror. I hate silence. I especially hate it when I know shit is about to go down.

I can't say that this should be easy, because I really don't want to jinx it. I know better. The world likes to throw shit at us just for laughs, and this doesn't feel any different.

"There's still no movement. Our guys are surrounding the entire complex," Beckett says, keeping track of the visual from the front seat. "We're going to be swift and quiet. There will be no prisoners. There will be no evidence left behind either."

This is really an act of war. We've done this before. It's nothing new to us. That's how Platinum Shores ended up in our possession. We helped Gilded Sands demolish a pack that was trying to take control.

"Ten minutes," Beckett adds, sitting up straighter in his seat. He flashes his open palm twice out the window, letting the others know.

I count my breaths and look at Holly, but she keeps her gaze trained on the windshield. She's just as tense as the rest of us, and I know that she's counting on us to be successful. There's no other option.

We can't let the Righteous Waters Pack interfere in our lives any longer. We can't risk them trafficking omegas. It's not right. They have been sentenced to death under our authority.

This isn't democracy. We can't have one until attitudes start to change. When alphas realize that they aren't what makes a territory flourish.

"Fuck. I have movement. Looks like someone is heading out. I can't tell who. They're wearing a baseball hat." Beckett unfastens his seatbelt, preparing to jump from the car as soon as we get to where we need to be.

"Don't make them rush, brother. One guy is nothing. We will surround him. He won't escape." Jordan cracks his neck, shaking out his body.

Beckett growls under his breath but he doesn't respond. He knows as well as anyone that Jordan is right. One guy leaving isn't going to change things.

Holly's phone rings, echoing through the air and startling her. She jumps in her seat beside me and scrambles to pull the noisy device from her pocket. I pat her leg, trying to calm her down. There's no reason to freak out by a noise. We're not sneaking into the building just yet. It's still a block away.

"It's the Pack Regimes," she says, staring at her phone

screen.

"Go on. Answer it." Beckett shifts in the seat. "We don't need them calling over and over again."

Especially because they don't call often. They usually communicate through messages.

Jordan slows down, turning on a side street that winds around the back of the complex, gated in with brick walls. It's a private apartment complex, and people need codes to get inside. It's made it easier to monitor.

"What's the emergency?" Holly asks, keeping her voice low. "It's unlike you to call."

"It seems we have a problem. There has been word that the Calico Proper region believes that your authoritative figures are crossing their borders. Do you know anything about this?" The familiar voice belongs to Spencer of Fire Valley, one of the desert territories on the other side of our region of Saint Vista.

"I have no—"

"You need to go back and verify they have your information correct, because we have permission. We have hired an outside security detail to join our court." Beckett grabs the phone from Holly with his lie, glowering at it like he wishes he could break it open and punch Spencer in the face.

"More security detail? I thought you had everything in control. You know you need permission from the leaders to bring others into our region." Spencer sounds annoyed, even more so than Beckett.

"We only needed two packs' approval, and we got it from Gilded Sands and Shadow Palms. It's not our fault that you were told otherwise," Beckett says. "So excuse us. We have to finish up our census."

Without waiting, Beckett hangs up the phone. He hands it back to Holly, his eyes narrowed with his anger.

Holly sighs. "That was definitely unnecessary. No other alpha would—"

A motorcycle revs its engine, drawing my attention to the outside of the car. That's when I see Andrew aiming a gun at a man with a baseball hat.

The guy raises his hands, standing straighter.

Fuck.

What the hell is going on?

"Is that Spencer?" Holly asks, digging her fingers into my thigh.

"Jordan, drive," Beckett commands. "Now!"

We don't get a chance to move away from the curb before several men in uniforms rush from between other cars, coming from houses outside of the apartment complex.

"Get out of the vehicle," Spencer says, a smile creeping over his lips.

It looks like Righteous Waters has already gotten to a member of the Pack Regimes.

This is worse than a trap. This is betrayal.

Never Break

HOLLY

"**A**lert my broth—" I startle as Spencer raises his gun and shoots, giving a warning shot.

I should've known that a neutral leader of the Pack Regimes could be persuaded to turn against me. He only cooperated with the shift in power because he had no choice otherwise.

And I'm pissed. He and his pack have put on an act that could fool the world. It fooled me. I've only ever been annoyed by his smug attitude. He was always first to tell me to settle down like I'm some sort of disobedient omega.

"Get out immediately or the next one goes into Jordan's head." Spencer saunters forward, smiling wider.

My stomach churns. Just the thought of Jordan getting hurt leaves me breathless. Protecting my pack is the most important thing in the world. I'll let Hector escape if it means no bloodshed will occur with the men I love.

I slide closer to the door, holding one of my hands in the air. "I'm coming. You don't have to act rashly."

Beckett growls deep in his throat, hesitating in the front seat. We have no time to discuss things or figure out a plan. And before I even get a chance to touch my hip, Spencer grabs my phone and tosses it. A few of his pack members surround the rest of my guys and take all their electronics away. The motorcycles clatter to the ground, and I'm shoved away from the Jeep, now remaining idling in the middle of the street.

"It has come to my attention that you have been performing unauthorized arrests. I felt it necessary for the safety of the Pack Regimes to intervene. You have started a war during a time where we're just mending from another. And frankly, I'm tired of the Gilded Sand predecessors causing so much trouble for the rest of us. Things were fine the way they were. But then you had to step up, trying to fill a position you do not belong in. You need to understand your place and take it without intervention from your brothers or the Silversteins."

Spencer tips his head as he studies me, getting close enough into my personal space that I can smell the onion fragrance of his nature. It's stronger than ever, and I know it's because I've stopped taking the suppressant pills that have helped diminish my innate senses as an omega. Some alphas that have once smelled good now smell incredible, especially Beckett and Andrew, but the alphas that I didn't really have a particular opinion about now smell disgusting.

I gag and cover my mouth. "What do you expect to get out of this? You're one person and there are many other leaders, including my brothers. Don't you think they would disagree with your opinion? This is treason."

Spencer surprises me by tightening his hand to the back of my neck and squeezing, forcing my face to his. Tears burn my eyes but not because I'm afraid. Because his stench makes me nauseated. His touch grosses me out.

"Get your fucking hand off her," Beckett says, shoving the beta that tries to restrain him. Jerking his neck, Beckett bashes his head into the man's, sending him to his knees.

The others take his place and grab Beckett, shoving him to the ground, aiming a gun to the back of his head.

"No! Don't hurt him!" My voice cracks with my scream.

Spencer raises his hands, stopping his men. "Like I was saying. I'm in control now, princess. You need to tell the Silversteins to settle down and to behave since they obviously have been pussy whipped into listening to an omega."

I gasp a few breaths and nod my head, turning to look at Beckett, Jordan, Isaiah, and Wesley. They all kneel on the ground now, scowling and looking like they are about to destroy the world. If only it wouldn't result in their deaths. I turn my attention to Andrew, who quietly stands with his hands on his head beside Dale. The two of them are not seen as a threat because they're not part of my intended pack. They don't know Andrew and I are starting to build a relationship with each other. That we all agreed that he is meant to be part of my pack, with all of us taking our territory name of Platinum Shores.

"Please, listen to them. Don't fight. It's not worth it. They know they have fucked up and will only hurt you. Just comply." I swipe my hand across my face, ensuring that no tears from my fear escape. I will not cry. I will not bow or break.

If only I believed that. My brothers have taught me that ever since I manifested as an omega, but it's hard to believe it in this reality. In this moment, when everyone looks down at me.

"Good," Spencer says when no one moves or argues. He turns back to me, loosening his fingers on my neck just a little. "Now to answer your question. The Pack Regimes will not disagree with this because I've already thought things through with a more worthy pack. You will renounce your reign. You will tell everyone that you are unfit for leading a territory."

This fucker. Of course, he'd command me to do something like that. My brothers already know I've been struggling with all of the constant battles for power. They've already heard from Beckett that he wasn't sure if he could do this. It would be believable if I told them that I no longer wanted to reign and that Beckett and his pack agreed.

It's in this moment that I realize I'm not a hero. I will not give up my pack to ensure my territory is safe. I have to do this. As much as I want to ensure that every omega is treated as they should be, I can't stand the thought of my guys getting hurt or worse. It's not a life I could live through. I'm not a perfect queen. I'm not a good person. I have blood on my hands just as they do.

"You will kill them whether or not I do," I say, my voice low. If I raise it any louder, I know it'll crack again.

"Now what kind of man would that make me? I know better than to do something so rash. If we were to kill them, then everyone would know. I prefer to do this in a more amicable manner. The war can end here. You'll give up your territory, and kindly pass it over to me to do as I see fit, which means fulfilling the restitution the Righteous Waters Pack deserves, and you can run home to your brothers and be the good little omega they never taught you to be with your men. Or you can continue as you are now without them. It would not be my fault if Righteous Waters retaliated for what you have done. I'm sure that some of the other leaders of the Pack Regimes would agree. The fact that you've heard this—make your choice, princess." Spencer smirks at me, his cocky attitude boasting with his pride. He thinks he's won. And maybe he has.

Because there's nothing I wouldn't do for the Silversteins.

"Holly, he's lying. He's not going to keep us alive." Beckett grinds his teeth with his comment. "Don't give up the territory. People need you."

I blink rapidly, my emotions trying to get the best of me. "And I need you." Turning to Spencer, I yank away from him and raise my head. "If you hurt them, I will kill you. Don't think I'm not capable. I will address the Pack Regimes, and I expect to have them back immediately or else you will be found out. And enemies of mine are enemies of my brothers and all our allies."

"If they behave, they will be fine. You have my word. The Righteous Waters Pack will not touch them as long as you fulfill your end of this agreement." Spencer looks to his men. "Take them away. Leave the bodyguard. Gilded Sands will know something is wrong if he is not there."

A bit of hope ignites inside me, watching as one of the betas pushes Andrew forward. That means I don't have to do this alone. We can get out of this. Spencer is an idiot if he thinks he can just take something that doesn't belong to him.

I just have to hold onto my faith that the Silversteins are strong enough to pull through. I know that they sometimes doubt their capabilities, but I believe in them. They just need to hang on.

"I want a second with the Silversteins," I say, fisting my hands.

"Only the alpha," Spencer says, spitting with his words.

I gulp a couple breaths, anger rolling through me and giving me the strength I need to step forward. Beckett glowers at me as if complying with Spencer is an act of betrayal. And if that's the case, then it is what it is. I'm not going to be the cause of our destruction. I will not let them be a martyr.

I won't be one either.

I quickly step close, getting on my knees because Spencer's pack doesn't pull Beckett to his feet, enjoying seeing him beneath them. I wrap my arms around him and hug him close, pressing my lips to his ear.

"Everything is going to be okay. Listen to me. Spencer won't get away with this. I need you to do as I say. I know you want to protect me, but you have to let me protect you." I kiss his lobe, feeling him shiver.

"Holly, please. Don't do this. They will not keep their word. I know men like them," Beckett murmurs, his muscles tense.

"I know, but you still have to trust me. Just don't do anything that gets you hurt, okay? Trust me." Hands lock in my hair and yank me from the ground, and I scream out and thrash.

It sets off the Silversteins, and it takes me screaming again for them to stop to get Spencer's pack to back off and not hurt them.

Spencer sets me on my feet, keeping his hand locked around my wrist. "Remember, princess. We're watching you. I have access to everything in your territory. You might have broken your alpha leaders, but I have my own. Just because Platinum Shores wasn't part of Saint Vista before doesn't mean I didn't have allies in Calico Proper. There's a benefit to being neutral."

He might not have had allies in Saint Vista, but it's obvious that he has allies in Calico Proper. It's not unheard of for regions to make ties. It's what keeps them safe from wars against each other. And I'm sure Calico Proper took a good look at Saint Vista when we were destroying ourselves.

Everything is starting to make better sense.

No wonder it was easy for Hector to get into my territory to mess with me. No wonder some of the alpha leaders continue to push back. They thought that my reign would be short, especially if another one of the leaders of Saint Vista's Pack Regimes was giving them that sort of hope. Spencer is probably the one that also ensured Righteous Waters' freedom. They have connections. They almost got me from Gilded Sands and created a partnership with my wretched father.

It feels as if he still wins in the end. He wanted me to be a broken omega like my mother, and here I am, facing the same fate. And this time my brothers can't intervene because they don't know.

The weight of everything lies on my shoulders.

But I won't let it push me down.

Alphas are nothing without omegas, and I will prove it.

I will not back down. I will not bow.

Nothing can shatter me.

Never Broken

HOLLY

"I have eyes on them," Andrew says, fisting his hand and pumping it. He's been talking to several people across different territories, getting the information he needs to hack into our own system that Spencer has locked us out of.

I snatch the phone away from him and stare at the screen, pinching my fingers to adjust the magnification. It takes everything in me to remain composed, staring at Beckett, Jordan, Isaiah, and Wesley as they sit against a plain wall in an empty apartment. Each of them has a bag over their head and their hands are restrained behind them, the position appearing achingly uncomfortable.

They probably will starve them and not give them a bathroom break either. As for the rest of our team? I have no idea. Spencer had Hector take Dale. I'm assuming they're either going to imprison them, torture them, or break them until they comply. I feel bad that anyone had to get involved. But we couldn't do it alone. Hell, we couldn't even do it with them.

Andrew rests his warm hand on my leg, drawing my attention away from the video feed and back to him, sitting behind the wheel of the Jeep. We thought it was best not to go back to the palace, but we also know we can't go running to my brothers in Gilded Sands. So now, here we are, trying to figure out the best way to approach things. I'm waiting for the rest of the Pack Regimes to respond to my emergency meeting. I don't think I can wait another day. I want Spencer to know that I will be a good little omega and step down immediately.

But I won't do it until I know my packmates are free.

"Don't worry, Holly. Our pack is tough. They'll manage until we can get them what they need. There will be someone willing to turn against Hector. I know it. He might think that his pack members are still loyal, but men like him don't earn loyalty. They steal it. They beat it out of people. If these guys think that Hector will be the death of them, one of them will turn their backs. We just need to figure out who."

Andrew's phone beeps and vibrates in my hand, and I spot a text message from an unknown number.

Without giving the phone back to Andrew, I click on the message.

Unknown: There is an omega male passing as a beta on the Righteous Waters Pack.

My eyes widen with the message. That's unbelievable.

I tap my finger across the screen.

Me: Does Hector know?

Unknown: No. It is the youngest of the pack. His nephew. His sister died just after giving birth, and Hector stole his nephew from her pack. After Righteous Waters was arrested, the nephew manifested as an omega in prison. Omegas aren't housed with alphas or betas. They ended up releasing the nephew to his mother's pack. They've been helping him by giving him suppressants all this time, and then when Hector was released, the nephew had to go back with him or risk him going after his family.

I stare at the text message in complete shock, my mind reeling. This is exactly the information we needed.

I bounce in my seat, hope blooming through me. Turning to Andrew, I cup his cheeks and kiss him. "Who is the source?" Because I want to reward them. They deserve the wealth of their dreams. They deserve strong allies to our pack. This information is miraculous. I had no idea. Not when I was betrothed to Righteous Waters. Not when they were framed for my death and went to prison. I guess only the nephew knew.

"It was easy to find someone from former Righteous Waters territory who hated Hector. Actually, he has a horrible reputation and they celebrated when he went to prison. The guy was one of his former leaders. I guess Hector murdered his brother." Andrew remains expressionless with his words. "When you lose your pack, you kind of gravitate toward people who have experienced the same. We have a mutual friend."

I hate that it took a tragedy to create something good, and I feel so deeply for Andrew in this moment that I kiss him again, showing him the affection he craves, my body turning wild with an unbidden need. Slick pools between my legs, and I pant, the Jeep suddenly suffocating me.

Andrew flares his nostrils, groaning under his breath. Pulling away, he gives me a once-over. "We need to get moving. Demand the Pack Regimes meet us immediately. I think you're going into heat."

What? Just hearing the words out loud startles me. I thought it was just about lust. I've never been in heat because of the suppression pills, and I don't really know what to expect.

"No," I say, my denial getting the best of me. "I just stopped taking the pills. It's going to take a bit of time."

Andrew squeezes my knee. "The scent of your body says otherwise."

My mouth rumbles. "Then we need to get our pack back now. I can't do this without them. I've never been in heat before."

Andrew blinks a few times. "Never?"

I shake my head and lick my lips. The more I think about his words, the more aware he becomes of my body. Maybe it was the trauma and the adrenaline that helped me ignore it, but now that the thought is fresh in my mind, I realize the subtle changes with me. How Andrew smells stronger. Better. And how awful the other guys, especially Spencer, smelled. And now my legs shake, my stomach twisting. I expect there to be pain soon enough, but no pain will be stronger than the ache in my chest. My need to find the Silversteins and bring them home.

"It's fine. I'm fine. Let's just get moving. We need to figure out how to get in touch with Hector's nephew." I rub my palms on my legs, trying to rub away the sweat. Damn. Kinsey wasn't kidding when she told me that it goes from annoying to intense pretty quickly.

"I'll drive, but you need to look at the feeds. This will be the best way. We'll just find him and take him. I doubt they'll be focused on him because they have other matters. I'm sure Spencer will have them busy." Andrew puts the Jeep into drive, pulling away from the curb.

I huff out a breath, trying to settle my nerves. I hope this is quick. I hope this is easy.

But I know that kind of hope is fleeting.

Nothing will ever be so simple.

"Yeah, he's in the database. I can send his information to you ASAP," a deep, rumbling voice says. I'd recognize the man anywhere. He's Mr. Donahue, one of the distributors of suppressant pills. My brothers have a history with him, and I know he wouldn't do something to warrant their wrath. Not after they gave him everything he could want.

"Thank you. You can check your account. Don't tell anyone." I quickly hang up the phone and lean back in the seat, wishing I were anywhere else besides this damn vehicle. I'm uncomfortable. I just want to cuddle up in my nest and hide for the rest of eternity.

But I have to keep pushing through. I don't have a choice. I refuse to go through my heat alone with only Andrew. I need

Beckett. I need Jordan, Isaiah, and Wesley. I just need peace.

"It looks like Jose will be due for a refill soon. I'm going to bribe him. It's the best I can do." I wiggle, my body begging for me to give it my attention.

I feel sick. Tired. I just—

Fuck me.

"I don't even think you'll have to do that, Holly, his order is a secret." Andrew's jaw twitches.

He knows how I feel about outing someone as an omega. It's completely wrong. I would hate for someone to do that to me.

But what else can I do? He's right. It would be much simpler.

I open the message on Andrew's burner phone, pulling up the information Mr. Donahue has given. Jose's address is listed in Calico Proper with City Dynasty as his home territory. This must be his mother's pack.

"The number listed is a different area code. Do you think he has a secret phone?" I ask, hovering my finger over the number, ready to click it.

"Possibly. The only way we'll find out is if you try. It'll be quicker than locating him with the feeds." Andrew turns down another street, keeping us moving. The last thing we need is to become an easy target. I don't know how many people are in on staging a coup with Spencer.

I'm usually not so anxious about calling someone, but what if we're wrong about Jose? What if he immediately tells Hector and they hurt my pack? I don't know what I would do if that were to happen. I don't think I'm strong enough to burn the world down. I'd prefer to help it thrive and grow. I'm not an alpha. Spencer was wrong about me pretending to be one. I will prove it.

Saying a silent prayer to the universe, I hit the number and clutch the phone. My heart races. It rings and rings, and I worry that Jose won't answer. I wouldn't. Not from an unknown number. If they want to talk, they'll leave a message, is my motto.

But I can't do that.

"Hello? Hold on. Don't hang up." The soft, masculine voice whispers. "I need a minute."

I reach out and grab Andrew, gripping his leg. I can't believe Jose answered. What if this is a trap? Maybe that's why he's making me hold on. He might be looking for our location, and assume that...no. They can't be like that. That's too much paranoia on my part.

"Hello? Lana, are you still there?" Jose asks, his voice low.

Lana? I wonder who that is. I've never heard that name before, and I wonder if Jose uses his phone to contact his mother's family. His family. I'm sure Hector would never allow him to see them, especially if he ever found out he's been lying to him this whole time about his order.

I clear my throat. "This isn't Lana, but please don't hang up. I'm begging you. You need to hear me out."

Silence greets me, and I'm not sure if he hung up after all, my pleas falling on deaf ears.

"Tell him who you are," Andrew whispers, slowing down to pull into an empty parking lot. "Just get to the point. It's easier that way."

I swallow the burning in my throat, my anxiety causing unbidden tears. "This is Holly. I'm sure you know why I'm calling, and I suggest you hear me out, considering that I know you are passing." I feel terrible even saying the words out loud. For some reason, murdering assholes doesn't feel as bad as threatening an omega who isn't much different than me. He has been dealt a shitty situation and he's doing what he can to make it through just like I did by faking my death.

"I don't know what you're talking about," Jose says, his voice deepening. "It's dangerous for you to call. If Hector finds out—"

"Then he'll know the truth about you. And I really hate that I have to do this, but I need your help. Don't you want to live a life without worry? Without having to hide from your own flesh and blood because of the order you manifested into? This is what I've been trying to do. Your uncle has been nothing but a brutal monster his entire existence. If you think for one second that he isn't, then you should just open up to him. All I'm asking is for your help. I need to be able to send a team in to retrieve my pack. You don't have to be involved after that. I can protect you. I don't know what you think will be accomplished by your uncle working with one of the Pack Regimes, but they're going to get nowhere. I promise you that. This is your chance to put this all behind you."

A soft growl reverberates through the phone. "I don't want to be in the open. I fucking hate that my body betrayed me."

"Do you know why?" I ask, keeping my voice soft, hoping that he continues to hear me out. It's a miracle that he hasn't yet hung up. "It's because of alphas like your uncle. They have instilled in everyone's heads that omegas are only good for one thing. But that's not true. Alphas are nothing without us. Don't you get that?"

"Nothing has been done to prove to me otherwise," Jose says. "I'm sorry I can't help you."

"Jose, wait. Please. I'm begging you. If you do this for me, you can have whatever life you'd like. You won't go down for Hector's crimes. You'll be able to find a pack who respects you. Please. You have to help me. Think of all the omegas that will fall by the hands of alphas if you just continue trying to pass as someone you're not. I've been there. It can't last forever. But this reformation I'm trying to accomplish will. There is no other option for me." I dig my fingers harder into Andrew's thigh, begging the universe for Jose to hear me out.

"I thought you were stepping down. You could just step down and get your pack back. I don't even have to be involved if you just—"

"You know they'll never allow it. I need this as a guarantee. Please." My desperation clings to me, sending my heart beating rapidly.

Jose doesn't respond for a minute, and I glance at the phone, nervous that the line disconnected. But he's still there, the timer ticking along as fast as my heart beats.

"Holly?" Jose asks, his voice shaking. "I'm afraid. If I get caught..."

"It would be better to get caught now than in the future. Don't you think? Hector is not a good man. The rest of the Righteous Waters Pack are despicable and undeserving of their name. I'll protect you. My team will ensure you are safe. I just need you to get them in. Will you do that for me, Jose? This is bigger than them just being the ones I love. I need them to help me with my position of power in my territory. They are important. And so are you." I open my eyes and glance at Andrew, meeting his gaze as he stares at me intensely, his eyes locking me in place. I wish I could dive into the depths of his gaze and lose myself in his soul. I need the comfort he brings me to engulf me, protecting me from this existence.

"So all I have to do is get them in?" Jose's words hum in my ear.

I nod even though he can't see me. "Yes. I will handle everything else. Make sure to pack a bag. You will be gone before your uncle even knows what happened. We'll all be free."

24

Rise Up

ISAIAH

"**J**ust a bit more. I almost got them." I growl under my breath, twisting and shifting my wrists, rubbing them against the binds. Whoever tied the knots in the ropes didn't do a very good job, probably because we're surrounded and can't exactly just make a run for the exit. I can hear voices outside of this uninhabited bedroom of the dirty apartment.

"Be careful, Isaiah. There are cameras. If they see you move too much, they'll come and check on us. It's best if they stay busy. We need to give Holly time." Beckett rests his head against my shoulder, acting as if he's exhausted. I know his adrenaline runs rampant, and it's taking all his strength to not thrash and fight. He's angry that we are in this position, and while so am I, I'm thankful that Holly isn't here with us. I'm grateful that Righteous Waters was too ignorant to see that Andrew might already be madly in love with her even if he hasn't admitted it to any of us yet. He's already agreed to a future with us. It's what gives me hope. Because Holly will make sure he is strong. She will ensure that everything ends up in our favor. That's how much faith I have in my beautiful omega. Nothing can get between us. We didn't get this far just to have the world strike us down.

Fuck that.

"I don't want her being put in danger. We need to figure this shit out before she is forced to step down. I know that they won't return us so easily. They'll want to make sure all remains quiet until they figure out how the hell they're going to deal with everyone else." Jordan speaks through his teeth. I doubt the camera in the corner can pick up every single sound in this room. Especially over the loud talking in the hallway.

"I agree with Jordy. I think it's possible that they'll take advantage of the situation and do something to Holly after she tells the Pack Regimes. They can make it look like we ran away or some shit. I don't know. It's hard to predict, considering that Wilder and his brothers would immediately know something was up. We just need to break out of here and start throwing hands. All we need is one weapon. One can turn to many more. You know this, Becks." Wesley rolls his shoulders, pulling against the ropes around his wrists. He thunks his head against the wall and peers at the ceiling. "I'm not afraid of getting hurt. They won't kill us until they get their way with Holly. We can't just sit here and act like fucking victims."

I pull harder on the bonds, stretching my arms until they ache. The ropes finally give way and loosen, allowing me to pull my hands free. I swivel and pull out my arm, wiggling it in front of my packmates. "We aren't fucking victims. And I don't care if they come running in here. I'm not afraid of them. I'm more afraid of what could happen to Holly."

I might not care, but I'm not stupid either. I'll do what I can before they realize what is happening on the camera.

"Hell yeah, Isaiah. Hurry up. Do Beckett next." Jordan squirms, trying to maneuver his own hands free. I'm sure with enough time we all could, but time is limited. I don't know how many hours have passed since we were brought here, but I know Holly would demand that the Pack Regimes meet quickly instead of tomorrow.

I scooch closer until Beckett leans against me completely, and I slide my arm around his back, finding the end of the rope.

He shifts more, and I say fuck it and use both hands, quickly loosening the poorly done binds, freeing him.

Glancing at the camera, I watch it for a moment, quietly listening as the voices outside the door fade.

Something is happening. I wonder if the dickwads have been called away to plot our demise.

Because obviously they had to see us getting out of our restraints.

Right?

I test my theory and flip off the camera, scowling at whoever watches us from the other side.

"Hello?" a soft voice whispers, static coming through the air. I realize that it must be a two-way sound system, because the voice comes from the camera.

The four of us freeze in place, staring at the blinking red light.

"Come on. Hurry," Jordan says getting to his knees.

I rush him while Beckett takes care of Wesley, and we quickly free ourselves completely. I stretch my arms over my head and roll my shoulders, my body aching from staying in the same position for what felt like eternity.

I head toward the door and touch the handle. Pressing my ear to the wood, I listen for the voices that have been nonstop since we've arrived. Again, I hear nothing.

"Can you hear me?" a voice says from the camera again.

Beckett strolls toward the camera and crosses his arms. "Who is this?"

"Thank God, you can hear me," the guy says without responding to Beckett's question. "I managed to freeze the frame. The others have gone to grab some food. You have five minutes to get out of the apartment. Head right and you'll find the rest of your team two doors down. Holly arranged for someone to meet you down the block. This is all I can do to help you. Hurry now."

The camera stops blinking, and I look toward my pack-mates.

"Do you think this is a trap?" Wesley asks, bouncing on his feet like he can't stay still.

Jordan pushes me out of the way and grabs the door handle, swinging it open. "I'm not contemplating bullshit. Whoever was on the other end mentioned Holly, and I trust our girl has shit handled. Let's go."

The bastard is right. I have faith in our omega and queen. The perfect ruler of our territory and pack.

Beckett follows behind Jordan, and I nudge Wesley to shadow him as I take the back. It's always been my job to watch their backs, and I take the job seriously.

It's how this has always been for us.

"If you see any weapons—"

"Hey!" a masculine voice yells, coming from a different bedroom.

I duck and charge, not hesitating as I shove a guy into the wall, knocking him down. He doesn't even get the chance to react as I pummel him in the face, punching him again and again until blood coats my fingers. He would do the same if he had the chance. I know it. I've fought guys like him before.

Beckett touches my shoulder. "He's down. Grab his gun. We're running out of time."

Shaking my head, I pull myself together and do as Beckett commands, fighting the guy's gun out of his holster. I pat down his body and find a knife, and I hand it to Beckett.

At least two of us are armed. It gives us a real fighting chance.

I check the gun, making sure it's loaded, and keep my fingers on the trigger. Moving forward, I get behind Jordan and back him up as he opens the door. I aim my gun, looking at our surroundings.

Pulling the trigger, I immediately shoot the guy standing outside the apartment, dropping him dead to the ground before he can even realize what's happening.

Righteous Waters truly thinks highly of themselves if they only have one guy standing guard out here. It helps if they underestimate us. Probably because Beckett is our only alpha.

Sometimes it's good to be thought of as less, so we can prove them wrong. We are stronger. We are more powerful. Claiming Holly as our omega already proves it. We have power that these assholes can only dream about. They weren't worthy before, and they're still not.

And I'm ready to make them see it.

"We're not showing mercy," Beckett growls, striding by my side. Wesley takes the end position, now holding the gun he took from the guard outside.

We stay together in formation, jogging the few dozen feet to the apartment two doors down. Wesley fires his gun from behind me, and I watch a figure drop to the ground in my peripheral vision. A man wasn't at the door, but he was running back.

"They know we've escaped," Jordan says, glancing over his shoulder at the rest of us. "There will be more coming."

Hell yeah, there will be. I don't know how many of Spencer's pack are here to stand beside Righteous Waters, but it will be more than we can handle.

Jordan reaches the door first and kicks it open without testing the doorknob. I aim my gun at an empty foyer and charge ahead, glancing around the unfurnished apartment.

"Looks like they were really depending on Holly to be compliant," Beckett mutters, moving ahead of me. I fall back beside Wesley, keeping my attention split between the front door and the bedroom where Beckett kicks open the door.

He and Jordan disappear inside, and I bounce on my feet, expecting an army to come running in to recapture us, beat the shit out of us, and make us pray for death. But I'm not fucking dying today. I would not abandon Holly that way. I'm certain enough that the universe has finally deemed me worthy of her, giving us the chance we need.

Beckett whistles, and I turn to him and frown, not liking his expression.

"Fucking monsters," he says, jogging past me. Jordan doesn't meet my gaze, his eyes wide and his face losing color. I don't have to ask them to know that the rest of our team, the guys that trusted us to help them make it out of here alive, are already dead.

I fist my hand and punch the wall, leaving a crater behind. I wish it were Hector that I could beat the shit out of. Those men didn't deserve such a fate. No wonder there was only one guard. Hector and Spencer thought our break-out team was dead. We will use their arrogance against them.

"Come on. There's nothing we can do. Our priority is Holly. We need to get out of here for her." Wesley motions for me to follow them, and I take my position at the end once more, wishing that Hector would show his face. I want to see his anger before his fear. I want to be the one he sees last before he finds himself burning in hell.

Another part of me is grateful that he's not though. No one else tries to stop us, either having some good sense or they just know they've lost.

My breathing quickens as I spot the side of the complex, and a vehicle idles just outside the wall.

"Lilac, what the fuck?" Beckett asks, grabbing our sister and pulling her into his arms. "You shouldn't have come here."

Lilac quickly pulls away and slaps her hand on the hood. "You know these misogynistic alphas don't give two shits about female betas. Of course I'm here."

"Get in, assholes," Ginger opens the driver's side door. "Our queen gave us a mission, and we're not going to let you guys mess it up. Now get in back and duck down. There are soldiers everywhere."

Damn. Spencer has already taken over our territory.

No one steals what belongs to us. No one destroys the work we put into turning this territory from a shit hole and into paradise. And no one messes with my omega or pack.

I'm going to make him pay.

25

Heating Things Up

HOLLY

I dig my nails into my palms, the ache between my legs growing worse by the minute. I don't know how I've managed to get myself into the building and to my private apartment within the leader tower.

My heartbeat thumps quickly, banging against my ribcage in an attempt to break free. I don't know how much longer I can stand this. I tried to take a suppressant pill, but I threw it up. It's as if my body completely rejects my attempt to stifle my coming heat. I know it's not quite here yet, but it could be any hour. Any minute even.

I need to get it together.

"Holly, did you hear me?" Andrew touches my shoulder, startling me from my thoughts. "The extraction was a success. Lilac just notified me."

I swing my gaze to Andrew, my whole body retching with my emotions. I sob and throw my arms around him, wanting nothing more than for him to hold me. This is exactly what we wanted. What we needed. I wasn't sure if Jose would come through for us, and I'm so thankful that he has.

But this isn't over. Just because my pack is free doesn't mean anything. Because Spencer is still in power and Hector is still out there.

I can't fathom going another day knowing that they're not snuffed out of this existence.

"You don't have to do this meeting now. We can tell the others what Spencer has done. You need to be somewhere safe and comfortable. The fact that you're sitting in room, in pain and crying, it hurts me. I feel so useless." Andrew rubs his hand over my arm, his skin caressing mine igniting fire inside me.

I whimper uncontrollably, burying my face harder against his chest. "I'm okay. We do have to continue with this. It might be my only chance to get within reach of Spencer. I can't trust the rest of the Pack Regimes either. I need to prove my point."

"Then let me help ease the ache. Just for a moment. We can't go in there until you can get yourself together." Andrew pulls me closer until I'm sitting on his lap, and he engulfs me completely, hugging me so tightly that my trembles disappear.

Easing back only a few inches, he tilts his head and kisses my cheeks, working his way from one to the other, brushing his lips against my sticky tears.

"We're going to get through this, okay?" Andrew murmurs, tucking my pale blond hair behind my ears. "Just take a few breaths. Our pack is safe. We're going to take care of everything. But let me take care of you first."

My mouth trembles and I kiss him, accepting his affection as if it's the one thing that will revive me. The one thing that will return my strength when my very soul is exhausted.

Gliding my tongue over his, I kiss him deeply, tasting the sugary sweetness of his mouth, craving for more. It's as if he put a cork on my fear and suppressed it enough to get me to focus on more than my dark thoughts. Now I imagine what it would be like to be with him. How good he would treat me. How amazing I'd feel.

"You smell so good," I whisper against his lips, rubbing my hands down his broad chest until I reach his belt. His bulge presses against me, his desire clearer than mine.

Andrew eases me off him and onto the couch, kneeling

between my legs as I lie vulnerable and aching, the position igniting a feral need.

"I know if you let me, I won't want to stop. So I'm just going to taste you for a bit. I'm going to ease away your ache with my tongue until I can have you fully and completely." Andrew's voice deepens with his lust, and he slowly leans over and hooks his fingers around my waistband, sliding my pants down and pulling them off. My slick dampens my body, and he flares his nostrils, sucking in a deep breath of my scent.

His muscles flex and move, his veins cording like ropes in his arms, traveling up his neck where his jaw remains tight as he clenches his teeth. I'm sure it takes everything in him not to rip his clothes off to sink inside me.

"I need more," I whisper, my voice coming out as a whine I can't control.

He closes his eyes and swallows, resting his palms on my knees, his hot skin igniting a delectable fire across my skin that travels to my very core. "I know, Holly. And I want to. But we need to just help you with your pain. Just hold onto the fact that when this is over, you're mine."

I smile at his words, my heart lifting with his affection. I never imagined I'd have another alpha outside of Beckett, and it feels so incredible to be loved even more than I already am. I'm so grateful to my pack for knowing what I needed before

I even knew for myself. I love that we are building something incredible and that we will fight to keep it. To make it better. People will try to stop us, but we won't allow anyone to get in our way.

"Speak up if you like something or don't. I'm here for you. This is about your pain and pleasure. Your body, mind, and soul," Andrew continues, slowly tugging down my panties until I'm left half-naked and exposed before him.

I squirm under his attention and arch my back, lifting my hips, my body begging for him to continue. He starts slowly, kissing my knee and working his way up my leg and to my thigh. The sensation sends explosions over me, his lips like a detonator, setting my body off.

I close my eyes, focusing on the sensation of his mouth, his tongue gliding across my folds until he spreads them open and flicks his tongue over my clit. I gasp and shut my thighs, squeezing his head between my legs. He doesn't stop, purring at my reaction. There's something about the way he holds me still that gets to me in a good way. His scent wafts around me, turning me on even more. God, his mouth feels so good, his lips pursing over my body as he gently sucks my clit into his mouth, massaging it with his tongue. Bringing his hand up, he slides it inside me, in and out, rubbing my inner wall until tingles burst across my insides, intensifying the pleasure he's awakened inside me.

"Don't stop," I murmur, combing my fingers through his hair, rocking my hips a bit to feel his hand more inside me. He slides in a second finger, the pressure building in intensity. I wonder what it would be like if he climbed on top of me. If he were to knot with me.

My eyes roll back at the fantasy, my muscles spasming as the ache pulses into undeniable bliss, my orgasm ripping a scream from my mouth.

"Fuck!" It's the only word my mouth thinks to say, whole body clenching, my legs tightening even more. Andrew would allow me to suffocate him with my thighs if it were possible, but he manages to shift his mouth just a bit, letting me ride the wave before returning right back to my clit, licking it with a bit more pressure now.

"That feels so good," I whimper, knowing that he plans on giving me another one. He wants to guarantee that the ache goes away for at least a little while. At least until we get through the meeting with the Pack Regimes.

My slick wets his face, the scent of our mingling desire permeating the air in a way that pebbles my nipples, and I rub my palms over my breasts, wanting to feel every sensation. Every ounce of pleasure.

I can only imagine how intense this will be when I go into

full-blown heat. It's almost unimaginable. My body already feels wild and insatiable. It takes everything in me not to beg him to fuck me. To give me his knot. To feel what it's like to be bound to him in a moment of intimacy. A moment of bonding that will tie us together.

Because I know Andrew is different. He wants me on the same level as the Silversteins. He plans to claim me the same way, promising me forever.

And that's exactly what I want.

Drawing his fingers inside of me, he presses against my wall, sending waves of electricity coursing through my body, zinging to my fingertips and my toes, to the top of my head and between my legs. I stiffen, my whole existence trembling with good anticipation, the orgasm even more intense, my body releasing all my pent-up emotions.

I squirt across his face, my slick soaking him in a way he clearly enjoys. Lapping his tongue across my skin, he tastes me, savoring exactly what he does to me.

I fall back against the couch, my body sinking into the cushion. Goosebumps prickle over my skin and I reach for him, wanting to feel the weight of him. Andrew shifts me over, laying on his side next to me, sliding his arms under and over me until I am pressed snuggly against his chest. Stroking his palm along my back, he smooths out my trembles, my body plunging from its high quicker than I'd like.

"You're so beautiful, Holly. You are so enchanting. I feel so lucky to even be blessed with your presence, and I'm so damn happy that you give me even a second of your time and body. I promise to always be the alpha you need. The alpha that our pack needs. I promise a world of love. A world where you no longer have to fear. I will not allow it any other way." Andrew's growly voice hums over my cheek as he brushes his lips to my earlobe, sucking it gently, making me shiver.

I believe him. I believe him with my whole heart and soul because I know he is capable. He makes me stronger just as Beckett, Jordan, Isaiah, and Wesley make me powerful.

Together we will succeed.

We are unstoppable.

26

Unstoppable

HOLLY

For the first time, I don't dress up like a queen in formal attire. People might refer to me as such, but I want to be seen as a leader. I want to be seen as someone who deserves this position compared to being born into it.

Everyone knows I wasn't. I manifested into a being without rights. A person who relied on her family to give her to another to take care of however they pleased.

My father betrayed me.

My brothers gave me a second chance.

And I have saved myself.

Now it's time that I saved my territory.

Adjusting my jacket, I smirk at the fact that I'm wearing pants. Andrew finishes lacing up my boots, not letting me dress myself. He claims it's an honor to have such a privilege, and I'll give him what he needs after our act of intimacy. Because my pre-heat has sent him into rut. He doesn't even want to leave this room, even though it's only a short walk to the elevator that'll take us up to the meeting room. He would prefer to stay here and help me create a nest of my own, even if this place isn't ideal.

But I'm okay for now. As long as I don't think about the ache in my body, I can step forward.

Straightening my shoulders, I peer at myself once more in the mirror and decide to take off my crown. I was going to do so in front of the leaders, showing that I'm truly renouncing my reign, but I don't want to give Spencer the pleasure. I want to make him nervous.

He will cower.

Adjusting my ponytail, I fix my long strands, hiding my decorative blade. There are no weapons allowed in the meeting room. Technically, no one should even be armed in this neutral territory. But we all know that's not the case.

The Pack Regimes only respect the meeting hall, and I can't

really blame them with people like Spencer lurking around.

"I'm ready," I say, tilting my chin down to look at Andrew as he kneels before me, still gazing at me as if I'm revered.

He clasps my hands and kisses my knuckles. "The others are waiting for your command."

I wish I had a moment to reunite with the Silversteins, but I don't want someone to accidentally find out that they're no longer imprisoned. We managed to cut contact within the territory, and Spencer has no idea. Hector won't be getting out. Jose has helped us ensure that all cameras remain frozen in time.

He's an angel, and I'm so happy to be able to give him the life he deserves.

"Good. I just want to get this over with and go home." I tug Andrew by his hands, waiting for him to get to his feet.

Standing up, he kisses my forehead. "That sounds like the best plan I've ever heard."

I gather my nerves and stroll from the small apartment, tangling my fingers with his, wanting to keep him close. No one knows that I have taken Andrew as an alpha alongside Beckett, and now is just as good as any to show it. I can't wait to see the leaders' faces. They thought that they could control who led by my side. But they can't.

Murmurs sound from the hallway, and I spot different pack

members from different territories hanging out in the lobby. Most aren't allowed to go in, and because Andrew was known as my bodyguard, it would be tradition for him to stay with them, but he won't leave my side. I won't let him. I'd like to see anyone try to tell me otherwise. Because I don't take orders anymore. I'm not going to just do as I'm told to please anyone.

I'm just as capable of ruling as my brothers. As the other alphas.

I'm also just as capable of shifting power once more.

This time there won't be mass bloodshed. This will be done quickly and quietly, handled discreetly. Word will not get out to the other regions. We will not be seen as incapable ever again.

I remain expressionless, keeping my head held high. I don't hide my gaze, and I look at each alpha and beta who tries to look at me. I spot a familiar face, and I wave to my cousin, who is head of security in Gilded Sands. I wish I could stop and talk to him, but I'm on a mission. I can't let anything distract me.

Offering him a smile and nod, I stride past him to the closed doors and press my hand to the palm pad, opening it. I've taken long enough that everyone should be here. I'm usually last anyway, my nerves getting the best of me.

Cool air blows around me, the fans pushing around every-one's scents, trying to keep them from lingering. It tickles my nose, and I try my best not to react. The stench of some of the alphas grosses me out, the intensity of the fragrance stronger with my pre-heat.

And then I see him.

Anger boils below my skin, coursing heat through my bloodstream. Hector shouldn't be here. He should still be trapped in my territory, which is now in lockdown. It's as if his presence implodes my entire life. How my brothers remain straight-backed in their seats is beyond me. I'm sure it takes everything in them not to cross the room to where Hector stands behind Spencer like a shadow.

"It's nice of you to join us," Spencer says, diverting his gaze to stare at Andrew clasping my fingers. "What is it that is so important that you have called us from our territories when we have a meeting scheduled for tomorrow."

This fucking asshole. He knows how to act, and I'm sure he will keep it up for as long as he can.

I step forward, training my eyes on his, refusing to look at anyone else. My brothers try desperately to get my attention without calling my name. I need to do this alone. They have gone through so much already, leaving them out of it is the best possible thing I can do. Because now I can show everyone what I am capable of. What I can handle.

"My first order is that I'd like to announce the addition of

Andrew onto my pack along with the Silversteins. We are to wed immediately." I smirk at Spencer, watching as his face twists.

Hector growls from behind Spencer, drawing attention to himself. "That bitch is mine. We had a deal."

My heart skips a beat, and I bite the inside of my lip to stop my reaction.

Wilder stands up and smacks his palms to the table, and Arsenio and Enzo join him, looking ready to lunge. Desmond must be with Kinsey, because if this was an emergency, they wouldn't have had time to plan security measures.

"What deal are you referring to? Holly belongs to no one. She is a member of the Pack Regimes, and frankly, I don't understand what that criminal is doing with you, Spencer. What is going on?" Wilder leans forward even more, his presence intimidating.

I remain standing in my place, giving each of the members a long look, wondering what is going through their minds. It's obvious that something is up, and it's making Spencer nervous.

"Spencer has demanded that I step down from my position." I narrow my eyes at the man.

He jumps from his seat, fisting his hands. "You're a fucking nuisance and a terrible leader. You allowed this man into our region. Your pack couldn't even handle his little threat. And now you try to frame me for your poor decisions? I'm a hostage. This man has some of my pack members imprisoned and threatened to kill them."

I open my mouth in exasperation. Spencer twists the whole situation to make himself look like a victim.

"Arrest him," Armand says, remaining in his seat. "We do not tolerate this sort of behavior. If you so much as hurt Spencer's pack, you—"

Lunging forward, Hector reaches for Armand and snatches him from his chair, yanking him back. He drags him across the floor and to the corner of the room, his hand laced around his throat while his other one rests on the side of his head.

"Tell him the truth, Spencer. We had a deal. Holly would be mine along with the Platinum Shores territory. We were to be allies. You were supposed to make her step down so I could step into her place." Hector flares his nostrils, his anger morphing his face with lines of rage.

"He's lying!" Spencer says, standing his ground with his story.

"What!" Hector shoves Armand into the wall, hitting his head against it.

Everybody stands up as he falls to the floor, knocked out from the gesture. Reaching into the front of his jacket, Hector pulls out a knife. I expect him to run toward Spencer, but he bolts directly toward me. No one tries to stop him, choosing to protect themselves, except for my brothers. They're just not quick enough. Andrew pushes me out of the way protectively, acting as my shield. He dodges out of the way of the blade, getting a snag on the front of his shirt. Shadows crawl along the edge of my vision, my body cooling, the pain inside me turning feral.

Oh shit. Not now. Please, universe. Not now.

My heat hits me hard and fast, the sensation shocking as agony courses through me, starting from my middle and working its way over every molecule in my body. I thought I could make it through this. I thought I could—

I hit my back against the wall and bow forward, the ache inside me worse than anything. I just want it to stop. I don't feel well. I feel not only sick to my stomach but sick to my soul.

It's enough to distract Andrew, and he glances over his shoulder at my cry. Hector doesn't relent, swiping his knife again. Andrew drops to his knees and shoves himself into Hector's legs, knocking him off his feet. His knife clatters across the floor, and I stare at it, my muscles frozen.

"Kill the traitor," Spencer says, rushing to grab the blade, but he's not quick enough. The fight blocks his way. "He'll destroy us all!"

No one knows what's going on. Arsenio rushes to me, trying to pick me off the floor. Hector trips him, growling and spitting, turning rabid with his fury. Scrambling forward he clutches the blade and swings, keeping the others away. Andrew acts as a shield between me and that monster, but he doesn't relent.

And I'm pretty sure he catches the scent of my heat, his eyes narrowing, focusing on me. He shoves Andrew, using all of his strength to knock my mate into the wall beside me, stabbing the knife at him, hitting the wall an inch from his side between us. I can't focus on anything, the commotion growing louder. Rumbling.

Wilder manages to grab Hector by the back of his shirt and yanks him away. Jerking his head, Hector butts my brother in the forehead, putting space between them. It's all he needs to lunge at me. Andrew jerks forward, knocking into the wild alpha, but instead of falling backward he falls away from me.

A hand locks around my ankle, and I jerk my attention up, staring straight into Hector's evil eyes. "You fucking bitch. You ruined everything. I'll—"

Blood spurts from Hector's neck, Andrew shoving the blade through the back of it. His eyes dim and he slips face first on the floor.

He's dead. He's finally dead.

I rest my back to the wall, heaving a breath. This isn't over. I know it's not.

Tears burn my eyes. I can't speak. I can't do anything but clutch my stomach.

Andrew touches my cheek.

Spencer materializes over us.

He smiles.

Long May We Reign

HOLLY

"What a magnificent fighter," Spencer says, placing his hands on his hips. "You saved us all."

My brothers rush toward me, ignoring the alpha, and I grind my teeth, my voice refusing to come. I want to beg them to kill him. To protect me like they always have.

"I think we all agree that your wish is granted. Andrew may lead with you in Platinum Shores." Taking a step forward, Spencer remains confident. Touching something inside of his jacket, he slowly pulls his hand free. I stiffen, but it's a phone.

Pulling it out, he taps the screen a few times. "As for the Silversteins...where are they?" he asks, continuing to remain expressionless. He's taking advantage of the situation. The Pack Regimes will have to decide to believe him or me, and I'm afraid that apart from my brothers, everyone will stand by his side.

"You know where they are," Andrew growls, speaking for me. "You're a traitor."

Raising his hand to his heart, Spencer touches his chest as if the accusation pains him. "I don't know what you're talking about."

"Righteous Waters." My voice comes out breathy, my whole body out of whack. It hurts so badly, sitting here so vulnerable before people who should never see me this way.

"What? Righteous Waters has them? I told you that they were trying to use me. I was being held against my will. They have some of my pack too." He really won't give up the act, and a quick look at some of the others, I'm starting to think that they'll believe him over me. Because why else would Spencer do this when he's been considered neutral for so long? He kept back and let others handle their territories and agreed with the new stipulations without argument. He has been seen as good. So why would he suddenly just change? They will believe that Righteous Waters had something to do with it.

"Oh dear. We need to send out a search team. Where did he encounter you before, Spencer?" This comes from Cameron. "We will get your people back. They will pay for this."

I squeeze my eyes shut. "He's lying."

No one acknowledges me, and I'm not even sure if I said the words out loud.

Andrew scoops me into his arms, lifting me from the floor protectively. He sees where this is going too. The last thing he wants is for shit to go down.

"He's a fucking liar. He's been helping Hector with someone from Calico Proper. They managed to infiltrate Platinum Shores and took the Silversteins hostage. He demanded that Holly step down." Andrew moves a foot closer but still keeps space between us. I know he's just trying to stand taller than Spencer, looming over him.

Spencer takes an automatic step back. "I told you. I was coerced." He continues to glance down at his phone, tapping at the screen.

I squirm in Andrew's arms, wanting nothing more than to slap Spencer. The lying bastard. The conniving asshole. How dare he use this against us. I will not let him win.

"Liar," I say louder, landing on my feet. My anger pushes me through the pain of my heat. The pain of being put in this position in the first place. The pain of nearly losing my pack.

Losing my territory. Losing fucking everything.

"She's delirious. Can't you smell her filth? She's gone into heat. This is why she can't be one of the leaders. She's incapable of handling anything." Spencer covers his mouth, acting as if he can't stand even breathing in the same space as me. Silence falls over the room apart from the low growl from Andrew. My brothers stand close, but they don't intervene. They wouldn't unless it was a hostile situation. They know better. They know that I have to stand up for myself.

"Liar," I repeat. "You wanted to take my territory."

"Don't be foolish. You're not in your right mind. Why don't you just go back to the apartment until you're feeling better? It'll give us a chance to discuss what happens next. Because I demand that Holly steps down." Spencer taps his phone again. "It is for the best. If you want your pack—"

The door to the meeting room flings open, and I puff a breath of relief at the sight of Beckett, Wesley, Isaiah, and Jordan. They've made it. I'm so happy they're here.

"If I want my pack to what?" I ask, gathering my strength from the men who love me. The men who look like they are about to destroy Spencer on my behalf.

"You escaped," Spencer growls, stiffening. He glances around the room, freezing in place as everybody turns from my pack to Spencer.

"Of course they escaped. You aren't strong enough to control us. You can't use my loves against me to put me in my supposed place. I'm the leader of Platinum Shores. I'm stronger than you, Spencer. I'm just as powerful as any alpha. Even more so. Because my pack makes me stronger. We work together to build a foundation. We are here for our people. We build trust. We don't take it. This is why I demand you step down. You are not worthy of ruling." My voice grows stronger and I take a step forward. I want Spencer to look me in the eyes and know that he has failed.

"She's telling the truth," a familiar voice says, stepping in behind the Silversteins. "My uncle and Spencer arranged everything. The Righteous Waters Pack wanted to take the Platinum Shores territory. They wanted revenge for making bad decisions and allying with the former king of Gilded Sands."

"Spencer, what do you have to say for yourself?" Cynthia crosses her arms over her chest, her face a mask of anger.

If looks could kill, Spencer would be dead. I wish he was already.

"I told you. I was coerced. You know me. I have been a part of the Pack Regimes for decades." Spencer bares his teeth, continuing to look around.

"Just tell the fucking truth!" I yell, my voice shrieking. All of my pent-up anguish explodes from me, and I charge forward and grab onto his shirt. "Tell them what kind of monster you are!"

Spencer shoves me, but he doesn't let me go. He grabs me by my neck, squeezing tightly. Andrew and Beckett grab a hold of him, trying to yank him back, but he doesn't let go. He would rather die trying to kill me than let me live.

I open and close my mouth, grabbing his arms, watching as Jordan pulls out a gun. He's breaking a rule that could get us removed from power, but I don't care.

I don't want to die.

My hand slips and I touch my hair, feeling the bedazzled hilt of the small blade. I forgot I was wearing it, tucked away in my thick strands.

Yanking it free, I swing my hand and stab Spencer as hard as I can into his ear, making him shriek. It's enough for him to let me go.

I gasp for breath, my lungs burning.

Agony tries to steal my consciousness, but I don't let it. I have to hold on. I have to prove I'm strong.

"This is treason! It is my right to demand a death sentence," I say, my throat hurting.

No one responds.

Jordan pulls the trigger, putting Spencer out of his misery.

Silence surrounds us.

The Pack Regimes stand in their place, and my brothers rush to me, joining my pack to check me over.

I keep myself together, holding back my burning tears. I need to address the situation now. I can't just let my alphas whisk me away. I can't allow my brothers to speak on my behalf.

My leg shakes, and I clutch onto Beckett's arm with Andrew by my side and Jordan, Isaiah, and Wesley standing around me, my protective pack stronger than ever. Because we know how to survive. We know how to fight. We know how to protect what is ours.

"This is my formal demand that we reassess everyone in this room. While we have made some progress, Spencer has proven that it's not good enough. Spencer's territory is mine as restitution, and I would like to have another pack of my choosing to run it. I'd also like to demand that we have more positions available for omegas and betas. Because clearly, having just me isn't enough. If you disagree, consider this war."

Am I crazy? Maybe. Or maybe I'm just tired. I have proven myself worthy of my position, and it is time that I get a say.

"Gilded Sands agrees," Wilder says, speaking up. "Alphas are nothing without omegas. We're nothing without betas either."

"As an ally, I agree as well," says Armand. "If war is necessary, then I will stand beside Platinum Shores."

Hope rises inside me. This is really happening. I'm making true change, and not just within Platinum Shores. I am changing all of Saint Vista.

"War is unnecessary. I agree as well," Cameron says, nodding.

One by one, each member nods their head in agreement, coming together in peace instead of letting this tear us all apart.

I almost don't believe this is possible, but a part of me knows that things can and do change.

If only there wasn't so much pain and suffering. Destruction and loss that forced everyone to truly see the world as it is.

But if we didn't see the darkness, we wouldn't be the light. We wouldn't be what the world needs.

"Let's all return to our territories and reassess everything to give Holly a chance to pick up the pieces of the recent attack and to take care of herself and her pack," Arsenio says, offering me a worried smile. Because my brothers will always be protective.

At least they know that they have done well. They have taught me everything I know, and I can truly handle myself.

Omegas can reign.

28

Bonded Forever

HOLLY

A whimper releases from my quivering mouth. My mind spins, my desire so strong that it's utter torture without the touch of one of my guys.

"She needs more," Andrew says, using his sleeve to dry my damp forehead.

"I'm on it. Fucking drive faster, Jordan. She's uncomfortable in the car." Isaiah grabs my hips, pulling me to his mouth instead of bending down. Beckett massages my nipples from beneath me, and Wesley offers me another drink of water.

Andrew and Jordan look ready to pull the car over to join us in the already crowded backseat.

"Two more minutes, my queen. Two more minutes and I will build you a throne of pillows. A palace of blankets. You'll have everything you could ever desire. Just hang on two more minutes." Jordan smacks his palms on the wheel, jerking the car forward, speeding too quickly to even see the buildings, the world a blur outside of us.

I arch my back and gasp a breath as Isaiah's tongue flicks over my clit, stroking me with enough pressure to help push away the pain of my need. Instead of trying to reach for him, I squirm on both Beckett and Wesley's laps, feeling the hardness of their bodies.

Turning my head, I grab Wesley and fight to pull free his cock. I just want to be filled completely. Though Isaiah's tongue brings me pleasure, I crave more. I'll die if I don't get more.

Pursing my lips, I suck Wesley into my mouth and moan, the taste of his pre-cum dripping on my tongue. He links his fingers through my hair and guides my mouth for me, treating me as his personal brand of ecstasy. It's what I crave. I want my guys to get off. I want them to fill me with their seed. I want it so badly that I feel as if I'll perish if I don't get it soon.

"Jordan, you and Wesley grab some supplies. Food, water,

towels. Blankets, pillows. Anything soft. Something that belongs to each of us. We need to surround her with everything that brings her comfort." Beckett reaches over and flings open the door for Isaiah, lifting me onto his shoulder to help keep me at his mouth. I've never had them pleasure me as we move from one place to another, and it feels so incredible.

"I need your knot," I complain, squeezing Isaiah with my thighs. "Where is Andrew? I need his too. I need to feel all of you guys come inside me. That's all I can think about. Please."

Jordan groans and kisses me from Beckett's arms. "I'll be fast, and then I'm going to work real slow. You're going to be screaming for days. God I can't wait to taste you again."

The world moves around me as Isaiah works his mouth over my clit until my body tenses and my muscles spasm, the orgasm helping to stop my aching pussy. But it won't last. I can already feel my need filling up once more.

"I got you, Holls," Beckett says, carrying me facing outward, his hand putting pressure between my legs, his fingers dipping inside me, slick with my juices. "You're going to sit on me okay? Andrew's going to knot with you first. You have to bond. Let him give you his mark. Let us use this as our bonding as a pack."

"I got your pants," Isaiah says, helping Beckett undress so he doesn't have to set me down. Andrew grabs at my top, my pants long gone. I don't even remember them coming off in the car.

Beckett's hot body envelops me from behind, and he doesn't hesitate, pressing his cock to my ass, my body so wet that he slips in so easily, the pressure zinging through me. His hand remains stroking me only for a moment longer until Andrew stands before me.

His beautiful eyes sparkle as he takes me in, watching as Beckett holds me still, his throbbing cock filling me in a way I'll think about forever.

"I love you, Holly," Andrew says, adjusting my legs off Beckett and spreading them wider, making it easier for him to stand close enough to sink inside me.

I scream out in ecstasy and grab his hips, pulling him as deep as he can possibly go. My body aches, but it's in a good way. Pleasure stanching out the pain, turning this moment into something beautiful. Something deep-seated and undeniably sexy. I can take care of my men just as they take care of me. And I've craved for so long to give them each a part of me, together, united as a pack.

"Goddamn. She's so fucking hot," Jordan says, his voice sounding through the air as he and Wesley come to us, standing beside Isaiah who strokes his own cock, naked and ready for his turn.

I lick my lips and wiggle my fingers, motioning him to come to me without my words. He perches one leg on the bed, getting his dick close enough for me to suck. I reach out and finally grab at Wesley and Isaiah until they each let me touch them with my fingers, all of them getting a part of me at once.

Andrew grunts, his knot swelling, locking me tighter, making my eyes roll until I'm floating in the world of pure pleasure. Pure lust. My orgasm controls every molecule in my body, Andrew's seed filling me how I need. The only way I feel as if I can breathe and feel as if I can continue on another moment.

Beckett strokes his fingers over my damp hair and kisses my cheek, not even caring that I am finishing Jordan off, his come filling my mouth.

"You're doing so good, Holly. So beautiful. I can't wait to fill you with my seed. I can't wait to see you swelling with our child. My beautiful omega," Beckett whispers his words, his fingers playing with my nipples, his body pulsing as he comes in my ass.

Andrew's knot loosens and he slides out of me, leaving me whimpering and desperate for more. He slides me off Beckett and turns me around to face him. Beckett licks my breasts and pulls me onto him, wanting to give me his knot next.

Brushing his lips to my shoulder, Andrew kisses me gently and swaps places with Jordan, letting him take his place. Jordan doesn't let him wipe off my body before he sinks inside me, moaning so loud, our voices a melody of our passion and love.

Each of my guys take care of me, kissing me and loving up on me. Taking turns using my body for their pleasure while ensuring that I get ten times more of my own.

Beckett tightens his fingers on my hips, bouncing me without lifting me, his knot swollen, the pressure intense in a good way. We can't move, but he continues to tease and test my body, our orgasms in sync, the warmth he puts inside me incredible.

Wesley enters my ass after Jordan, and Isaiah finishes in my mouth, the six of us enjoying every second of this.

And when we're all content, Beckett draws a bath, and the five of them help clean me, continuing to feed my need as an omega until I can't even keep my eyes open. And even then, they cuddle me for hours, keeping me warm and safe, showing me just what the rest of our life has to offer. It is so enchanting. Our life together is beyond my wildest dreams. I never expected to live a life of love and happiness. I never expected to live a life without being under an alpha's control.

But here I am, the leader of five men who would do anything for me. Five men I'll cherish forever.

They are mine. All mine.

The world will never get between us.

We are strong.

We are united.

And as a pack, we'll ensure the future is everything beautiful and blessed. The future will be perfect for everyone.

29

HOLLY

I can't believe it's been a week since I nearly lost everything, but it's also been a week since I got everything of my wildest dreams. My pack. My territory. Endless love and devotion and the capability of caring for omegas everywhere.

"You just need to sign your approval here, Holly. This will guarantee that all territories in Saint Vista will be ruled by a governing body united by love and power and not by individual leaders." Armand holds out a pen, and I stare at the documents with everyone's signatures scrolled across, changing the

Pack Regimes to the United Packs. We hope this will be the beginning of a change greater than our region. We are hoping this becomes worldwide, especially when other alphas see just how amazing our world can be with alphas, omegas, and betas working together peacefully and as one. No more power wars. No more games between leaders.

And most importantly, no more omegas being treated like property.

We have a right to live and love and choose just as everyone else does.

Nothing has felt more incredible.

Well, except knowing that my guys have taken on the new pack name Silver Shores to embody what we are all together. We don't need the reminder of the old territory Platinum Shores and how we got here. All we need is a change to better our future.

"We will also have the list of candidates by tomorrow morning. Each of us have submitted those nominated by the majority of the betas and omegas." Armand waits for me to sign the documents, and I set the pen down, a small gesture bringing me great relief.

Beckett rests his hands on my shoulders from behind me, squeezing me gently, his scent dazzling my senses, my body still running on a high from everything we've been through.

"Does anyone have any questions?" Armand asks, looking toward my brothers and the rest of the leaders, before returning his stare to me.

I shake my head like everyone else. This is the beginning of something beautiful, and with all of our insight and knowledge, our entire region will surpass everyone in the world. I just know it.

"I'm going to say this meeting is adjourned," Wilder says, scooping up the documents and putting them into a metal lockbox. It'll give us all the time to process things to ensure we don't need anything changed at the last minute. We'll reconvene in a week and look at the contracts with fresh eyes. It'll also be when we announce who will be joining the United Pack's governing body.

I stand from my seat and turn to find myself engulfed in Beckett's arms. Holding me close, he kisses my forehead before finding my mouth. I sink against him, savoring his affection, ignoring the rest of the room as the other leaders disperse. It's so strange to think that just a few weeks ago, very few alphas would even meet my gaze, and now they're respectfully addressing me, acknowledging my power, and treating me as their equal. I can't wait to see the change when our governing body flourishes.

"I'm so proud of you, Holls. My beautiful mate. My everything," Beckett murmurs, easing away to meet my gaze.

We now stand alone in the empty room, though muffled voices waft in from the lobby just outside.

I giggle and kiss him again, my heart and soul floating on the high of managing such an accomplishment—not making Beckett proud, per se but managing to keep my promise to my pack of a brilliant future. Also proving that an omega's reign doesn't end at the power of an alpha. It grows and strengthens. An omega's reign isn't some fantasy to be snuffed out. It's the beginning of the change the world needs.

"I couldn't have done any of this without you and our pack. We're a team. A family." I grin, my features crinkling with my happiness. I've never felt so incredible in my life, and I'm no longer afraid it'll end.

"You're absolutely right. Which is why...we want to make it official." Beckett spins me around, facing me toward the lobby.

My mouth falls open in surprise as dozens of people stand around, holding sparkling lights, bringing the stars right in front of me.

Andrew, Wesley, Isaiah, and Jordan stand at the end of a makeshift aisle lined with fabric-covered chairs decorated in flowers. They all wear tuxedos, looking so incredibly handsome. My brothers stand off to the side with Kinsey, the five of them beaming with love and pride. None of us grew up expecting such an incredible life, and I'm so happy to be able to share it with them.

A silver runner sprawls across the floor, the entire lobby decorated like a fairytale. Twinkle lights and flowers bring color and warmth to the starkly plain room, and I take a moment to appreciate the effort my pack put into this. They managed to do all of this in such a short time that I know they'll be able to accomplish so much over our lifetime.

"May I," Beckett asks, offering me his elbow.

I smile and walk toward the rest of our pack, my knees shaking in the best way. I had no idea something so elaborate was coming. I had basically demanded the acceptance of a proposal and union from the former Pack Regimes that I didn't think my guys would follow this tradition with the building of the United Packs.

"It is a great honor to have a beautiful, strong omega standing before us today," Andrew says, speaking to the crowd, watching in joyous silence. "It is also the Silver Shores Pack's honor to recognize our lucky stars in finding such an outstanding, incomparable mate and leader."

"One who offers us love and equality as a pack. A woman who I love waking up to every day to see by my side. A woman who doesn't want to conquer the world but wants to bring it together just like she has brought our packs together," Wesley says, holding out his hand to me.

I glance at Beckett with another smile, and he lets me go to the others, closing off the circle in which they surround me.

"Holly, no matter how many times I tell you this, I feel as if I can tell you a million more times. You make my life complete, and I love you so deeply and irrevocably that I vow to always protect you and treat you like the most important woman in the world that you are to us." Isaiah pulls out a velvet box with five glittering rings that will all fit together to make a beautiful representation of our pack on my finger.

"We promise to always treat you not only as an equal, but as a leader. I plan to worship every inch of you for the rest of my life and the rest of my eternity and you will always be happy and satisfied in my presence, and I will ensure the same for the others," Jordan says, gliding his tongue over his lips, setting off my lust.

I blush, the heat pooling in my cheeks sending my body buzzing. Giggling, I pat his chest, and he pulls me to him, our bodies flush together.

"I don't even care if there's an audience. We will take care of you in every way you need," he whispers, stroking his hand lower.

"You're too much, but I love you. I love you all." I spin in a circle, giving each of them my attention.

"And we love you too. Our devotion is endless, and we promise the future of our desires. We vow our loyalty and our everything to you and this pack, Holly. Will you grace us with your love and bond for the rest of time?" Beckett takes one of the rings and slides it onto my finger, our hands joining together as one, our fingers and palms pressing so close that I can feel his very soul radiating from him.

"Of course. Yes," I say, tears brimming my eyes, my whole body filling with a wave of incredible emotions that I want to survive on.

Each of my guys adds a ring to my finger, and I open my arms and let them hug me between them. The room breaks out in cheers, and I snuggle my face to Andrew's chest, feeling Beckett behind me, and Isaiah, Wesley, and Jordan wrapping us all in their arms.

We have built our pack the way we have always wanted. No one chose us for each other. We have found each other and have brought our strengths together to be unstoppable.

And we will help others do the same.

Saint Vista will unite in a way no one has ever seen.

There won't be any more looking down on others because of their order. We will all learn to love and appreciate ourselves from this point on. Because we bring the best of everything when we join as a pack.

We bring love and laughter. Hope and promise. But mostly, we bring infinite possibilities.

No one will reign alone.

Because the world is better when we are all together.

We are all a pack.

A family.

We are all one.

30

Epilogue

HOLLY

The sun sets on the horizon, turning the sky beautiful, rich oranges and reds with streams of purple. Cool air plays with my blond hair, and I press my hands to the stone wall of the palace. Tonight marks a year since the Pack Regimes were disassembled and reformed as the United Packs, and it's almost hard for me to believe. I pinch myself every day, knowing that we have broken the generational trauma of our parents and all of our ancestors before us. We have healed our people, and now we strive to turn our stitched-up world into something only marked by scars. The scars that have and will always remain as a reminder of the life we never want again.

"My queen, come join the party," Isaiah says, still using a formal title as my nickname, because even though I'm one of many in charge, I'm his queen. No one else's but my pack's, the way it should be.

I turn away from the glittering ocean, the sun painting it in breathtaking warmth, and slide my fingers through Isaiah's.

He guides me toward the ballroom, where music trickles through the air, and hundreds of people enjoy each other's company. The scents of alphas and omegas and betas permeate the air, blending as one in such a way that in this moment, I can't tell the difference between anyone. And I love it.

My heart has never been so full as it is now.

I don't make it three feet into the room before Jordan slides across the floor and opens his arms, hugging his face to my stomach.

I laugh and comb my fingers through his hair.

"How is our baby and mama?" he asks, pressing his lips to the silky fabric of my ball gown.

Wesley strolls up with a plate of food. "Probably starved."

Beckett and Andrew join us, smiling as they also hold plates of food like it's a competition to feed me and the life I carry for the first time.

Because the fates chose now to be the perfect time for our pack to grow, giving us this whole year to work toward ensuring our future of stability and prosper.

I giggle and let Andrew feed me first, because he chose to sneak into the kitchen for the desserts, and I lick the sweet frosting from his fingers. "I am amazing. We're amazing," I say, smiling at each of my guys.

Beckett kisses the frosting from my mouth. "That we are. Always."

I smile. "Forever."

Thank you so much for reading Omega's Reign. If you haven't read her brothers' story, check out The Knotty Girls Club and The Knotty Princes Club!

OMEGAVERSE SERIES

Saint Vista Pack Regimes

Bonds of Steele Omegaverse

PARANORMAL

The Seven Sinners of Hell's Kingdon

The Pack Mates of Lunar Crest

The Wolfpacks of Shadow Moon Island

The Fated Mate of the Dragon Clans

The Divine Vampire Heirs

The Royale Vampire Heirs

The Academy of Vampire Heirs

La Vega Vampire Showstoppers

Rise from the Flames

About Ginna Moran

GINNA MORAN IS the *USA Today* Bestselling author of over seventy novels including the popular The Pack Mates of Lunar Crest and The Seven Sinners of Hell's Kingdom reverse harem novels.

She always carried a fascination for all things paranormal and wrote her first unpublished manuscript at age eighteen. Her love of the supernatural grew stronger through her adult life, and she now spends her days with different creatures of the night. Whether it's vampires, werewolves, dragons, fae, angels, demons, or mermaids, Ginna loves creating and living in worlds from her dreams.

Aside from Ginna's professional life, she enjoys binge-watching TV, crafting and design, playing pretend with her daughter, and cuddling with her dog. Some of her favorite things include chocolate, mermaids, anything that glitters, learning new things, cheesy jokes, and organizing her bookshelf.